She gripped her stomach. "Oh, no!" she cried out, doubling over.

"What? Sarah, what's wrong?" Case asked.

The pain intensified. "I think…oh!" she exclaimed, the pain gripping her tight. "I think…the baby's coming," she managed to say.

"Now? But you have weeks to go."

On instinct, Sarah knew the baby was coming early. And they were out in a desolate part of the range, with no form of communication. The baby wasn't going to wait.

"Babies don't always come on schedule, Case."

Case straightened and nodded, a determined light coming into his eyes. "Okay, okay. Let's get you into the car. We'll make it to the hospital in half an hour."

Sarah shook her head and grabbed on to his sleeve. "No, Case. There isn't time. The baby's coming too fast."

She met the fear in Case's eyes with her own. There was no way around this. Sarah knew what he had to do. The contractions were intense and coming far too frequently. She pleaded with him now. He was her only hope.

"Case, you have to deliver my baby."

Dear Reader,

Get your new year off to a sizzling start by reading six passionate, powerful and provocative new love stories from Silhouette Desire!

Don't miss the exciting launch of DYNASTIES: THE BARONES, the new 12-book continuity series about feuding Italian-American families caught in a web of danger, deceit and desire. Meet Nicholas, the eldest son of Boston's powerful Barone clan, and Gail, the down-to-earth nanny who wins his heart, in *The Playboy & Plain Jane* (#1483) by *USA TODAY* bestselling author Leanne Banks.

In *Beckett's Convenient Bride* (#1484), the final story in Dixie Browning's BECKETT'S FORTUNE miniseries, a detective offers the protection of his home—and loses his heart—to a waitress whose own home is torched after she witnesses a murder. And in *The Sheikh's Bidding* (#1485) by Kristi Gold, an Arabian prince pays dearly to win back his ex-lover and their son.

Reader favorite Sara Orwig completes her STALLION PASS miniseries with *The Rancher, the Baby & the Nanny* (#1486), featuring a daredevil cowboy and the shy miss he hires to care for his baby niece. In *Quade: The Irresistible One* (#1487) by Bronwyn Jameson, sparks fly when two lawyers exchange more than arguments. And great news for all you fans of Harlequin Historicals author Charlene Sands—she's now writing contemporary romances, as well, and debuts in Desire with *The Heart of a Cowboy* (#1488), a reunion romance that puts an ex-rodeo star at close quarters on a ranch with the pregnant widow he's loved silently for years.

Ring in this new year with all six brand-new love stories from Silhouette Desire....

Enjoy!

*Joan Marlow Golan*

Joan Marlow Golan
Senior Editor, Silhouette Desire

Please address questions and book requests to:
Silhouette Reader Service
U.S.: 3010 Walden Ave., P.O. Box 1325, Buffalo, NY 14269
Canadian: P.O. Box 609, Fort Erie, Ont. L2A 5X3

# The Heart of a Cowboy

## CHARLENE SANDS

Published by Silhouette Books
America's Publisher of Contemporary Romance

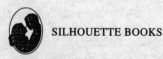

**SILHOUETTE BOOKS**

ISBN 0-373-76488-X

THE HEART OF A COWBOY

Visit Silhouette at www.eHarlequin.com

**Printed in U.S.A.**

**Books by Charlene Sands**

Silhouette Desire

*The Heart of a Cowboy* #1488

Harlequin Historicals

*Lily Gets Her Man* #554
*Chase Wheeler's Woman* #610

---

# CHARLENE SANDS

resides in Southern California with her husband, Don, and two children, Jason and Nikki. When not writing, she enjoys sunny California days, Pacific beaches, sitting down with a good book and, of course, happy endings!

She loves to hear from her readers. Contact her at charlenesands@hotmail.com or visit her Web site at charlenesands.com.

To my husband, Don, my best friend, my love and my own special breed of cowboy. Ain't nobody better, honey.

And special thanks to my talented editor, Patience Smith, for your effort in making this book come together. It's always a pleasure working with you.

# One

Case Jarrett pulled his truck up to Red Ridge Ranch and heaved a heavy sigh. He glanced at the ranch house he'd grown up in. After months away busting broncs on the rodeo circuit and silently grieving the death of his brother, Reid, he was back now.

Bounding out of the king cab, Case lifted his Stetson off his head to run a hand through his dark hair. Arizona heat coiled around him like a diamondback snake tightening about his body. He welcomed the familiar swamping and took in a deep breath of dust-laden air, then returned his hat to his head.

He had a promise to keep and wondered how Sarah, his brother's widow, would react to his moving back home. Hell, he'd debated his decision over and over in his mind and hadn't come up with any other way to protect his family home and keep the promise he'd made to Reid on his deathbed.

Case had kept his distance for five months—since the funeral—but Sarah was eight months pregnant now and Case couldn't justify his staying away any longer. He was needed here. Always had been. Guilt yanked at him hard. If he'd been here, seeing to the Triple R, helping out, maybe Reid wouldn't have died so tragically. His brother would still be alive to witness the birth of his first child.

Instead Reid was buried in the family plot five miles up the road. Case had stopped by on his way in, noting the fresh batch of wildflowers on his grave. Sarah, no doubt, had laid down those flowers. When the front screen slapped open, Case snapped his head up. Sarah stood on the front porch, just outside the door and her expression, that momentary sign of hope, slammed into his gut. Disappointment registered quickly on her face when she recognized him. Being an identical twin brother had had its share of benefits at an earlier age, especially where Sarah was concerned, but now, his very appearance was a constant reminder to her of the husband that she'd lost. She did a fine job of covering up, but Case knew beyond a doubt that for one instant before reason and reality set in, Sarah thought she was seeing the man she had married.

*Take care of Sarah for me, Case, and the baby, too.* Reid's dying words echoed in his head. He'd made the promise while Reid was drawing his last breath. But Case hadn't stayed on too long after the funeral. He'd headed back to the rodeo straight away.

Sarah was in good hands, he'd told himself. Her sister Delaney and her two young daughters had come to spend time on the ranch, keeping Sarah company, helping her cope with her loss and the pregnancy. Case knew she'd been taken care of then, but summer was over now and

Delaney was gone. She'd taken her children back to California when the new school session began.

A hefty dose of conscience had struck Case while pulling back a pint of Jack Daniels and he'd called Sarah from Denver one night. She'd been crying, but darn her stubborn pride, tried her best to disguise it. Sarah Johnston Jarrett couldn't lie worth a damn.

Case knew then, he had to come home. For Sarah and for Reid. The irony was, that for all his good intentions, he now had to come face-to-face with the woman he'd been avoiding for the past six years. The woman he'd secretly wanted. The only woman in the entire state of Arizona who could make him break out in a sweat with one pretty smile.

Case had his share of beautiful women, but no one compared to Sarah, in his mind. He'd envied his brother but never once begrudged Reid his happiness. Reid deserved every single ounce of joy he could attain. He'd been a good man, solid, dependable, a man Case had been proud to call brother.

If only Case had stayed on at the ranch.

But Case couldn't live under the same roof with Sarah. He couldn't afford for anyone to find out, that Case Jarrett, ladies' man and all-around bad boy, had fallen hard for his brother's girl. The day they married, Case took off, leaving the ranch, claiming a need to sow his oats and ride rodeo.

"Hello, Case," Sarah said, from just outside the front door. She moved to the porch post and leaned against it. She was heavy with child now and her movements seemed labored. There would be no grand greeting for him, no happy welcome home. He couldn't say he deserved it, either, but often he wished just once, Sarah's eyes would light for him, the way they'd always done for Reid.

"Sarah," Case said, nodding and removing his hat.

They stared awkwardly at each other for a moment. Then Case lifted his boot heels and headed her way. Red dust swirled under him as he ate up the yard with long measured strides until he faced Sarah. Her sweet flowery scent knocked his senses for a loop. How the woman always managed to smell so damn good, Case couldn't figure.

"What are you doing here?" she asked cautiously, checking him over from head to toe. "Did you get injured again?"

Case had come home from the rodeo circuit once when he'd busted his ribs from a fall off a feisty bronc named Dynamite Dan. That and for a few days during each Christmas were the only times Case had ever returned to the ranch.

He shook his head and lifted his arms out wide. "Nope. All in one piece this time." She didn't appear relieved. Instead her expression bordered on wary and he knew what question was on her mind—why had he come home? She wouldn't like his answer. She wouldn't take kindly to his return. And for Case, it wouldn't be easy living under the same roof with Sarah, wanting her the way he did, but an equal measure of guilt and honor had brought him home, for good. "Hey, how many babies you have in there?" he asked, glancing at her belly. "Last time I saw you, you could fit inside the barn door."

That comment brought a soft chuckle to her lips. Sarah was beautiful when she smiled. He'd have to get used to seeing those smiles on a daily basis and not react to them. He couldn't let Sarah know what one of her pretty little smiles did to him. "Only one, but he seems to be growing faster than Bobbi Sue's baby heifer.'' She placed her hand over her abdomen.

Case took in her appearance. Her eyes looked weary, the soft blue ovals were rimmed with red. Subtle contours of her lovely face appeared drawn and tight. And although her golden hair shone like sunshine, Sarah looked exhausted. "You feeling okay, Sarah?''

"I'm fine.''

"You're working too hard,'' he said, moving a little closer, getting a better look.

Her smile faded some and she took a step back. That was Sarah, always backing off from him, always wary. "I need to keep busy, Case, and there's lots of work to do.''

Sarah *had* been working too hard. Well, that was about to change. Case let his brother down once and that mistake might have cost Reid his life. Case wasn't about to neglect his brother's widow or his unborn child. Not again. He wasn't going to let Sarah work herself into the ground, either. He knew she had a stubborn streak. She was one determined lady who didn't back down from trouble.

And there had been trouble. But it hadn't been Sarah who had confided in him. No, he had to find out from Benny Vasquez, the neighbor on their south border, that Sarah had been threatened by pushy land developers to sell out. The woman probably thought she could handle the situation on her own. He hadn't given Sarah much reason to trust him, but damn it, he sure would've liked it better if she'd been the one to confide in him about what was going on.

Whether Sarah wanted him to stay on or not, he'd see to the trouble. Case would bet his championship belt buckle, Sarah wasn't going to be happy about it. Not one bit.

He rubbed the side of his neck and glanced her way. "Let me get the trailer unhitched and my bags unpacked and we'll talk."

Her light blond brows arched up. "Your bags?"

There was a look of panic on her face with that dawning knowledge. Couldn't be helped. Case's mind was made up. He and Sarah were going to live together at the Triple R, and both were going to have to deal with the consequences. "That's right. I'm moving back home, Sarah. To stay."

Sarah fidgeted nervously in the kitchen, strumming her fingers against the oak table and tapping her toe against the floor. She heard Case upstairs; slamming shut drawers, opening the sliding closet doors, whistling out a tune as he made himself at home.

She reminded herself, this was his home, too. He owned half of the Triple R, not that he seemed to care much about it lately. It appeared that the minute she and Reid married, Case was out the door, leaving his family home and his legacy behind. Reid had never complained, he just picked up the slack, but Sarah had often wondered why Case had left so abruptly. She couldn't help but feel she'd intruded on his life, barging into his home and taking over.

He said he was home…to stay. Dread crept up her spine. Case was a virtual stranger to her now. She'd hardly spoken to him in six years. She didn't know him anymore. How could she manage to live with Case, in this house, after all that had happened between them in the past? Sarah's stomach churned, a queasy feeling reminiscent of her early pregnancy. Only this time, it wasn't the baby causing commotion to her insides, but instead, the baby's uncle.

He was Reid's brother and he did own half of the Triple R, but Sarah hadn't given much thought as to what she'd do when Case decided to claim his half of the ranch. She certainly hadn't expected him to come home now. She knew he was riding high on the rodeo circuit, having won several bronc-riding championships. He'd been sending money, and that amount had doubled lately from his recent successes, to help with ranch expenses and Reid's hospital bills. The ranch was heavily mortgaged to pay those debts and Sarah honestly didn't know how she'd manage to pay off the loans. But one thing was certain, she wasn't going to give up on the Triple R.

With Case it was different. He'd seemed to lose interest with the ranch and as soon as he was old enough, he'd taken off. His sudden unexpected reappearance had really rattled her.

By law and by rights, her share of the ranch would belong to her child one day. Moving off this land had never been an option. She loved the ranch too much to think of leaving. The Triple R was home. But she never thought she'd live here without Reid. She'd never fathomed a freakish accident would claim her husband's life.

The raging dust storm that had spooked the animals and caused the barn collapse had nearly taken Reid, as well. A wooden beam from the rickety barn loft had struck him down as he tried saving the animals. He'd lingered for days, fighting off the crushing pain to his chest and Sarah had been by his side, holding on, listening as Reid uttered words of assurance. There had been silent understanding in his words, and Sarah's heart bled each time Reid would make plans for her future without him. In the quiet moments right before Reid's death, he'd said point-blank, the Triple R would be her home forever. Sarah had prayed for the best, but feared the worst. And then the worst did happen…his heart gave way. Reid died five days after the accident.

And now Sarah would be living with Case.

She heard footsteps descending on the stairway and stood up abruptly to pour the coffee she'd brewed. But the fast move made her light-headed and she swayed, grabbing for the kitchen chair.

"Sarah?" Case was beside her instantly, steadying her shoulders with strong hands.

The room spun, and Sarah took a deep breath. A moment later, her head cleared. She looked into a set of deep brown, concerned eyes. And her skin burned from the heat of Case's solid hold on her, his fingers gently digging in, reminding her what it felt like to be in a man's arms. Reminding her, what it had been like being in *his* arms. But Sarah didn't want to dwell on the past. She had enough to deal with, right now, in the present. "I'm okay. The doctor says not to get up too fast. My blood pressure's a bit low and quick moves tend to make me dizzy."

Case helped ease her down into a chair. "Sit down and take it easy."

"You don't know what you're in for, *living* with a pregnant woman." She couldn't believe what *she'd* be in for, living with Case, either. They both had some adjusting to do.

Case's eyes never left her face. He sat down across from her. "I've got a feeling I'm going to learn about it right quick. So, you don't mind me coming back?"

"What about the rodeo?" she asked abruptly. Of course, she minded, but she had no right tossing him out. He owned an equal share of the ranch.

He studied her face for a moment. "I'm entered in a handful more events so I'll go back from time to time, but this is my last year. I'm through. What do you say, Sarah? Can you abide me coming back to the ranch?"

She shrugged. What could she say? She couldn't very well kick him out. He'd left the ranch at a bad time. Money had been tight, beef prices down and they couldn't afford to hire on any more help. Reid had done the work of two men to make ends meet back then, but now, it was Case's turn to work the land, she supposed. "It's your home, Case. Reid would want it this way."

"But…not you?"

Sarah wouldn't lie. She had her doubts about these living arrangements. He was Reid's brother, but he was also a man Sarah couldn't trust. He'd let Reid down too many times. "Case, we hardly know each other anymore. At best, it'll be awkward."

"Sarah, listen. I need to be here right now, but you have my word, I'll stay out of your way. I know about the threats you've received." His tone sobered considerably and his expression grew fierce. His deep dark eyes penetrated hers with raw determination. "Nobody threatens a Jarrett."

"Case, they weren't threats really. Mr. Merriman from the Beckman Corporation got a little too…enthusiastic in his bid to get me to sell the ranch. His company is planning this big housing community called Beckman Bridle Homes and the Triple R seems to be right smack in the middle of where they intend to build."

"I heard the McPhersons refused the offer, too. Not too long after their barn burned down suspiciously."

"Yes, that's true. It happened last week, but they can't prove anything. Luckily no one was hurt. Seth McPherson spotted the fire and they put it out before any live-stock got caught in the flames.''

''You should have told me about this. I had a right to know.'' Anger burned low and intense in Case's dark eyes.

''I didn't think you'd...''

''Care?''

''Well, it's not as though you've taken an interest in the ranch, Case.''

''The ranch is my business now, Sarah. And you, living all alone out here.''

Sarah was alone now. And she felt it every day. She'd been lost when Reid died, and had to fight off her melancholy for the baby's sake. She'd never known this kind of loneliness before. ''There's more than half a dozen hands on the ranch. I'm not entirely alone. Besides, I handled Mr. Merriman in my own way. He probably won't be back.''

''How can you be sure?''

''You didn't see the look in his eyes when I pulled out Reid's Winchester and aimed it straight at his heart.''

Case's lips lifted in a small crooked smile and uncannily, Sarah felt that smile all the way to her toes. ''You chased him off the property?''

She nodded, remembering that day all too well. The man had been more threatening than she'd let on to Case. And he'd forced himself inside the house, using verbal pressure when she'd refused his offer of sale. What was worse, the man knew of the ranch's outstanding debts and that they were headed for financial trouble. He played on that until Sarah couldn't take another minute of it. She'd asked him to leave twice, before reaching for that rifle. ''You could say that.''

Case shook his head. "You won't have to worry about him again."

Probably not, she thought wryly, but now she'd have another worry. She didn't relish living with a man like Case. They'd had a history together that she didn't enjoy recalling. Growing up in a small country town, their paths had crossed more times than not. Case hadn't made her life easy. Two years her senior, he'd been a bully at times, a tease, and later when they'd been in their late teens, he'd played a trick on her. One she still smarted from.

One she had trouble forgetting. And forgiving.

Case Jarrett may have shared similar looks with her late husband Reid, but the differences between the two were clearly notable to her now. Oh, not physically, but Sarah couldn't help but look at Case and see the man who had abandoned Reid and the Triple R when he was needed the most. Sarah saw a man bent on danger. She saw him as the man who had tricked and cajoled her one too many times.

How Sarah had ever been fooled in the past by their identical appearance, she couldn't understand now. And the scar slanting down Case's cheek from his right eye only marked him as different to *others*…a way of singling him out from Reid. But to Sarah, Case was nothing like Reid, and she didn't need that facial wound to remind her that Case Jarrett was certainly not his brother.

"Is that why you're back, Case? Are you worried about the ranch?"

Case narrowed his eyes and drew in a long breath, deep in thought. "It's my responsibility now, Sarah."

She nodded, wondering why, after all this time Case felt the need to own up to his responsibilities. He'd never been the type to settle down. And if his coming back had anything to do with her, she needed to make one thing abundantly clear. "But I'm not."

"You're not *what?*" he asked, the picture of innocence.

"Your responsibility. I can take care of myself."

Case had the good sense to stifle a smug smile, but Sarah sensed she knew what he'd been thinking. She'd nearly fainted dead away just now from dizziness. And he'd been the one to catch her before the fall. "Tough pregnant lady, are you?"

"I'm a rancher's wife, aren't I?" At least she had been, up until five months ago. The heartache was still with her each and every day, but she had the baby to think about so she looked to the future instead of aching in the past. More than anything she wanted this child to thrive. Nurturing this baby was her only source of comfort.

Case nodded and averted his eyes. He stood then and poured coffee into a mug. "I've got to have a talk with Old Pete and let that crotchety foreman know I'm back at the ranch. I'll spend the day out on the range, checking over the place. I plan to do my share of the chores around the house, too, so don't you lift a finger on my account. I didn't come back home to add to your work. I'll be back in time for supper. I'm cooking tonight."

"You cook?" she asked, startled. Sarah knew Case was a capable man, but she didn't think of him being comfortable in the kitchen.

"Don't get too excited. I get by. My meals are edible, barely. I'll let you be the judge."

Sarah lifted herself from the chair, bracing a hand on the table for support. Case reached his hand out, but then quickly retracted the offer once Sarah had straightened without his help. "One chance is all you're getting, Case, so make it a good meal. The baby needs his nourishment. And I get real crabby when I'm hungry.''

"I'll make a note of that.''

Sarah watched Case leave out the back door then heaved a deep wearisome sigh. Case Jarrett was back. She'd have to get used to him being around, is all. There wasn't a doggone thing she could do about her circumstances. She and Case would be living under the same roof from now on.

Whether she liked it or not.

Case burned the steaks on the grill. The potatoes were choked with garlic and Sarah had never seen flatter biscuits. But she ate the meal without a fuss and listened to Case's assessment of how he'd like to make a few changes on the ranch.

He had ideas for saving money and time that Sarah thought sound enough. She agreed with him on some things and gave her opposition on others. Case listened to her quietly, nodding his head then strengthening his arguments to make her see things from his point of view. He had a stubborn streak that matched her own, especially when he believed he was right. Which was pretty much all the time.

When dinner was over, Case helped Sarah bring the plates to the sink. He rinsed as she loaded the dishwasher. At times they worked so closely, their hands brushing as he handed her one dish after another, Sarah felt the need to flee. She hadn't been touched in such a long time, and twice today, Case had touched her. Once to catch her fall and now this. It was silly to feel so awkward around him. She'd known him a long time. He was her husband's brother, uncle to her unborn child. But she also felt a sense of disloyalty, irrational; as it seemed that she was somehow betraying Reid by engaging in such domestic rituals with another man.

Get a grip, she warned herself, this is how it's going to be from now on.

Case looked around the kitchen, nodding his head, claiming that the dinner was a success and the room was cleaned. Sarah had to burst his bubble. Her baby needed more than meat and potatoes to survive and so did she. She cleared her throat and smiled sweetly. "Case, thanks for the meal, but I think I'll take over the cooking duties from now on."

Case stood with both hands on his hips, pursed his lips and studied her for a time. "Thank God," he said finally, surprising her.

"W-what? I thought you wanted to cook some of the meals?"

His lips parted with a devilish grin. "Hell no. I hate my own cooking."

"Then, why did you offer?"

"Seemed like the right thing to do, Sarah. You nearly keeled over right in front of me today. I was afraid my being here was an added burden to you."

That was true, but feeding him had nothing to do with it. It was the seeing him every night and waking up in the morning part of their arrangement, that Sarah disliked. She'd be living with her husband's brother, a man she didn't know all too well, a man she had a brief history with in the past. She'd put that part of her life behind her, only to have Case move in here and remind her all over again, about times she'd rather not recall.

And besides all that, she hated losing her privacy. She wasn't always at her best, being eight full months pregnant. Some days she just wanted to scream down the walls and others she wanted to cry until there were no more tears left to shed. It didn't set well that Case had to witness some of her less than perfect days. She was too tired to try to cover up her feelings from anyone, anymore.

"You made me eat charcoal steak and greasy potatoes, Case. That's cruel and unusual punishment. From now on, we'll have a well-balanced meal. The baby needs his vitamins."

"If you say so," he said, lifting dark eyes her way. She wore a pair of loose denim overalls with a tiny T-shirt top underneath. It was comfortable attire and she knew she must look like an overstuffed Mrs. Farmer John. Yet, his eyes traveled over her, grazing her with heat as he peered at her blossoming chest. Sarah had never been so well endowed. Her body was preparing for nourishing the baby and it appeared, Case had noticed. The appreciation she noted in his eyes brought forth tingles that ran the length of her spine. With one heated look, Case had the ability to make her forget she was eight months pregnant. With one look, he'd made her feel soft and feminine again.

Sarah cleared her throat. "I do. But tomorrow's dinner will be a little bit late. I've got a doctor's appointment in the afternoon in Prescott."

"Who's taking you?" Case asked immediately.

"Well, nobody. I'm driving in myself."

"Like hell you are. What time is your appointment?"

"Three."

"I'll take you."

"That's really not necessary." Sarah didn't understand Case's sudden involvement in her life. She'd made it clear that she wasn't his responsibility. She didn't want him watching out for her. She had to learn to get by without any help since she was going to be a single mother. Case was the last man she'd ever rely on. He'd proven time and again that he couldn't be trusted. "I'm perfectly capable of driving to town, Case."

He came up as close as he could get without crushing the baby and pinned her with a look. "And what if you get dizzy again? Then what?"

"I only get dizzy if I move too fast. And I'm being very careful about that."

Case blew out a breath and the classic Jarrett pig-headed expression stole over his face. Sarah knew she'd be better off agreeing, since no amount of discussion was going to change his mind and she just wasn't up for an argument. Having Case move back home had taken a definite toll on her today.

"Be ready at two, Sarah. I was meaning to get into town soon anyway."

"If you insist, but you don't really have to."

He grunted his reply and strolled out of the kitchen.

Case settled himself on the back porch steps and took a swig of his beer. The golden liquid slid easily down his throat and quenched his thirst. Stretching out his long legs, he leaned on his elbows and glanced up at the stars, but Sarah's image appeared, out of nowhere it seemed, and interrupted his peace. He'd been thinking about her all day. Couldn't rightly get her off his mind.

That night years ago flashed into his head, like a moving picture and plagued his memory. Sarah had looked so beautiful in her flowing pale blue gown, standing there on the threshold, expecting Reid to pick her up for her much-anticipated senior prom. Reid had come down with the flu, but hadn't wanted Sarah to miss out on the evening. He'd practically begged Case to don his rented suit and replace him for the evening. Case protested—he didn't want to go to some fancy doings with his brother's girl, but in the end, for his brother's sake, he agreed.

The mistake was in not calling Sarah first, to let her know the situation. Reid argued that she wouldn't go if she knew how sick he'd been, so Case agreed to tell her once he got to her house. But once he knocked on her door, Sarah gave him no time for explanations. The minute she saw him standing there in his brother's suit, believing him to be Reid, she flowed into his arms and kissed him soundly on the lips. Case hadn't expected the intense surge of passion that erupted within him. He hadn't expected to enjoy Sarah's lips moving over his or her sweet scent nearly buckling his knees.

On pure male instinct, he wrapped his arms around her and deepened the kiss, thrusting his tongue in her mouth. Incredible sensations wiped all rational thought clear from his head. He forgot all about his mission, the fact that Sarah could never be his.

They kissed deeply, Case pressing her back with small exquisitely sensual steps until he had her braced against the wall. Their bodies touched intimately, the whisper of satin crushed up against his groin. He couldn't hide his arousal. He couldn't get enough of her. He needed more, to touch her and continue touching her. He'd never been so taken by a female before. He'd never felt so overwhelmed and completely helpless to the sudden urges consuming him.

She arched back and he traveled kisses along her delicate throat. Her moans of pleasure caused him to throw all caution to the wind. He couldn't think beyond absorbing Sarah into his heat. Within seconds, her dress was unzipped and his hands found the contours of her smooth back, his lips the beautiful swell of her breasts.

She tasted better than heaven, better than anything he'd ever known. He wanted Sarah more than his next breath.

Intense desire seared through him like a burst of flames. He'd pressed himself closer and hiked up her pretty dress. The soft silky slide of her nylons gave way to bare flesh. She burned under his fingertips and moaned his name. *His name.* "Case, stop. You have to stop."

Startled, Case did stop, looking Sarah dead in the eyes. How long had she'd known it was him and not Reid, he would often wonder. Why hadn't she stopped him immediately?

Case slugged back another gulp of beer and shook his head, remembering. Sarah had been furious and called him every name under the sun. Denial played heavily on his lips, but he didn't defend himself, he couldn't. But to keep Reid from getting suspicious, he'd finally convinced Sarah to go to the party. They'd both agreed not to tell Reid what had happened and not to speak of it again. It was the only way Case could calm her down.

They'd spent an awkward tense night with Sarah hardly able to look at him. She hadn't let him touch her. They hadn't danced. Case knew Sarah thought he played a dirty trick on her. He couldn't blame her—he'd always teased and tormented her in their younger days often times pretending he was Reid. But Case had to let her believe that he was just plain rotten, that he'd used her in a mean-spirited game rather than to let on to the truth. Because the truth was far worse and it had hit Case right smack between the eyes that night. He'd fallen for his brother's girl. The girl Reid had professed to love since the age of fourteen. The girl Reid was going to marry.

Case cursed his bad luck and chugged down another swig of beer. The strong smell of liquor was soon replaced by a flowery scent that teased his nostrils as it drifted by.

"Case?"

Sarah's soft voice from behind had him swiveling his head. She stood in the doorway, dressed in a short white cotton robe. His gaze riveted instantly to her legs, exposed from the knees down. They were still shapely, regardless of her pregnancy and he recalled how damn soft they'd felt when he'd slid his hand up her thigh and touched her there. He wanted that again. He wanted to hold her, kiss her and finish what they'd started that night. Damn. His whole body tightened, just looking at her. "Huh?"

"I forgot to tell you at supper that you had a few messages. Penny Applegate, Josie Miller and Reba Stokely called. They'd heard you were back in town and wanted to say hello."

Case nodded and averted his gaze. The last thing he needed was to hook up with any of his old girlfriends. He'd had enough female trouble on the rodeo circuit to last him a lifetime. It'd be hell enough living with Sarah, much less getting involved with any other female right now. "What'd you tell them?"

"Only that I'd give you the message."

He nodded and lifted his eyes to meet hers. "Consider it done. You going to bed now?"

"Yes. Uh, well, good night, Case."

"'Night, Sarah."

Case listened as Sarah entered her bedroom and closed the door. Good thing she decided months ago to move into the downstairs bedroom, he thought earnestly. At least, he wouldn't be bumping into her in the middle of the night.

He finished his beer and rose slowly, trying to banish

Sarah and those torturous memories from his head. He cursed his bad luck once more, thinking of the lonely nights ahead and the promise he'd made to his brother. He'd take care of Sarah and the baby for as long as necessary and she'd never know why he'd really come home. Her stubborn pride wouldn't have it. Case knew undoubtedly if he'd told her of Reid's deathbed plea, she'd become indignant and refuse his help.

Case needed to do this. He had demons to chase and guilt to absolve. He wouldn't let Reid down again.

But it wouldn't be easy. Sarah barely tolerated him. She didn't want him on the ranch. And she didn't trust him worth a damn.

# Two

Case was used to fast speeds and quick action, but he deliberately took it slow with Sarah seated beside him in the truck. She sat as far away as possible and glanced out the window rather than make conversation with him. He knew he'd bullied her into agreeing to this, but darn it, she could grant him a smile once in a while, couldn't she?

"What's the doctor's name?" he asked.

"Dr. Michaels."

"Never heard of him," he said conversationally.

"*She* came to town about a year ago."

Case raised a brow. "She specialize in delivering babies?"

Sarah turned to him and nodded. "She's an OB/GYN, if that's what you mean. She has a great reputation. Reid and I researched all the doctors in the area and she seemed to have the best credentials. I have a lot of faith in her.''

''That's good, Sarah. When's the baby due exactly?'' he asked. He had one more rodeo event scheduled this month, but he wouldn't go, if it were close to the baby's due date.

''I'll know more after today's appointment, but Dr. Michaels thinks the baby will come in about four weeks.''

''You and Delaney go to those classes and all?''

''Yes. She took me to six childbirth classes. She promised to come back when it's time. She'll be a great labor coach, having gone through it twice already.''

Case shuddered at the thought of witnessing the baby's birth. Selfishly, he was glad Sarah had Delaney to rely on to be there for the delivery. Case had pulled many a calf and pony in his day, but it ended there. He knew nothing about delivering babies.

When their brief conversation died, Case glanced at Sarah out of the corner of his eye. So pretty, he thought, with her long golden hair blowing in the breeze. He witnessed her tucking the strands that had brushed her cheeks, back behind her ear. He wished he had the right to run his fingers through her hair, to let the golden lights play over his hand.

She was a feisty one, though, with her chin raised indignantly. She wasn't going to make today easy on him. But he'd secretly admired that trait in her. He'd put her through a lot as kids, but she'd never buckled under. One thing about Sarah Johnston, she always came out swinging.

The usual thirty-minute ride into Prescott took Case over forty-five, going ten miles under the speed limit, just to make sure Sarah was comfortable. He'd been careful on the pitted road not to hit any big potholes.

Once in town, Sarah directed him to Dr. Michaels's office building. She was nearly out the door, before he stopped the truck. "Thanks, Case. You can come by for me in about an hour."

"Hey," he said, bounding out of the truck in time to help her down. She hung on to his arm, mostly for balance as he helped her feet hit the ground. He'd like it fine if she'd keep her hands on him, but she pulled away from him real quick. "Not so fast. I'd like to come and meet the doctor."

"W-why?" she said, curiously.

"Why? This is the doctor who's going to deliver my nephew, isn't it?"

"Could be a niece, Case. We don't know for sure and yes, Dr. Michaels will do the delivery."

"Well then, I'm coming with you."

"But, I thought you had errands to run in town."

"That can wait. This is more important." Although the thought of the delivery scared the dickens out of him, Case was just plain curious about this whole birth process. He needed to understand things, like how would he know that Sarah was in labor? What were the signs? What if Sarah had trouble?

Another shudder ran down his spine. Damn, the whole thing made him jittery.

"I don't know, Case," she said, a doubtful expression marring her face. There was mistrust there, too, along with a large dose of reluctance.

"You can decide inside," he said, glancing at his watch, then taking her arm gently. "Or you might be late for your appointment."

Once inside the office, Case took a seat next to Sarah

in the waiting room. For all anyone knew, they must have appeared like a loving expectant married couple. Case breathed in her subtle flowery scent, noted her shapely legs peeking out from her pretty dotted dress and marveled at the serene glow on her sweet face. Damn, being near Sarah still had a powerful effect on him. If he could claim Sarah as his, he would and be done with it, and they'd really be the loving couple they seemed to portray. But Case knew beyond a doubt that would never happen.

"Mrs. Jarrett," the medical assistant called from an opened doorway.

Sarah struggled to rise. Case stood and helped ease her up slowly. He laid a hand on the small of her back and guided her to the door. She stopped and turned to him. Case didn't want to bully her again. This had to be her decision. "I'd really like to come in with you, Sarah," he said softly.

Sarah stared into his eyes for a moment and he noted wariness mixed with reluctance, but when she relented with a brief nod, Case felt a small sense of relief that he'd won this round with her. The medical assistant led them into a small examining room. There, the assistant asked Sarah to step up onto the scale. "Don't look," she said firmly, before she took off her shoes to get on.

Case stifled a chuckle and glanced out the window. "Wouldn't dream of it." He'd never understand a woman's vanity. Sarah was as big as a house, beautifully so, but still she worried that he'd find out how much she weighed.

After her temperature and blood pressure was taken, Dr. Michaels walked into the room and stopped dead in her tracks when she noticed Case. Confusion mingled with uncertainty and she gave Sarah a questioning look. "Mrs. Jarrett," she said, darting a glance from her chart to Case and back. "I'm sorry, I was under the impression—"

"Oh," Sarah said quickly, "this is *Case* Jarrett, Dr. Michaels, my husband's brother."

"Identical twins?" she asked, realization dawning instantly.

"Yes," Sarah answered.

Case put out his hand. "Pleased to meet you."

After blinking once, Dr. Michaels took his hand. "Nice to meet you, too. Are you planning on attending the birth, Mr. Jarrett?"

"No, he's not," Sarah put in. "My sister will be here for the delivery. You might remember her. She took me to all my appointments during the summer."

"Yes, I do remember her. Well, then, let's get started. You're due for an ultrasound, I see."

After the doctor did an assessment of Sarah, checking, measuring and answering her questions, the assistant brought in the ultrasound machine. "Here we go," Dr. Michaels said, once Sarah was all hooked up. "You might want to stand a little closer to Sarah's side of the bed, Mr. Jarrett. The screen isn't very large."

Case positioned himself by Sarah's side and watched in utter fascination as the doctor applied a jellylike substance to Sarah's abdomen, then moved an instrument around slowly. The picture on the screen appeared to take form and Case witnessed a miracle in the making. Awestruck, he asked Dr. Michaels, "That's the baby?"

"Uh-huh, but the little babe doesn't want to turn so we can see the sex. Healthy one, though."

"Are you sure, Doctor?" Sarah asked, motherly concern apparent on her questioning expression.

"He looks fine to me, Sarah. The baby's got a steady strong heartbeat."

Case watched the baby move around on the screen. He glanced at Sarah, captivated by the look of joy and serenity on her face. He was so moved, he had to put his hand on her shoulder. Surprisingly she reached up to touch his hand. The contact ripped right through him and the solid rhythm of his heartbeat went a little crazy.

"He's beautiful, isn't he, Case?"

"Couldn't agree with you more," he said, completely taken by the moment. "He's so small."

"But it doesn't feel that way to me," she said softly.

"No, I don't suppose."

Case cleared his throat, humbled by what he was witnessing. "But he or she is keeping us in suspense. Don't know if we should paint the nursery blue or pink."

Sarah slowly lowered her hand away. "The room is yellow and green, Case. Delaney and I already painted it."

The magic of the moment was suddenly gone. Sarah had made herself perfectly clear. She wasn't including him in with her plans for the baby. He couldn't say he blamed her, with him showing up spur of the moment and expecting...what had he been expecting? He knew damn well Sarah wouldn't welcome him home. But he was the baby's uncle. He did have some rights in that regard.

"I'd like to speak with Dr. Michaels privately now, Case." she said gently.

He nodded. "Sure thing. I'll be in the waiting room."

Dr. Michaels shot Case a thoughtful expression, then handed him a brochure about what to expect when the baby comes. "Here you go. Interesting reading, when you get the time."

"Thanks, ma'am," he said, grateful for small favors. "Appreciate it."

Case sat in the waiting room staring blankly at the brochure. For a minute there, he thought Sarah was softening toward him. They'd shared a moment of sheer joy and fascination, witnessing the baby make its subtle movements. Case had never experienced anything quite so awe-inspiring. And the look on Sarah's face was worth a thousand eight-second rides.

From behind, he heard Sarah's voice. She was making her next appointment at the reception desk. Case stood and faced her. She smiled tentatively and he walked toward her.

"Ready to go?" she asked.

"I'm about famished. C'mon, we're going out to dinner. Anywhere you want."

Case silently groaned when Sarah suggested a diner notorious for health food salads and soy dishes. The lady certainly wasn't going easy on him. No sir. And soft sweet Sarah knew exactly how to hit a man below the belt.

He put a hand to her back and led her out to the truck. *"Tofu Sally's,* it is," he said, unruffled. "I can hardly wait."

Sarah shuffled her salad around on her plate, aware of Case's eyes on her. He'd been watching her intently as they sat at the diner and ate their meal. He'd already polished off two veggie sandwiches without complaint and was working on peach pie with two scoops of some soy concoction of ice cream.

"So, the good doc thinks the baby will arrive right on schedule?" he asked, after taking in a forkful of pie.

"Yes, four weeks and counting," she replied.

"And Delaney will be able to get away in time?"

"Yes, she's going to leave the girls with her neighbor

during the day. Her husband Chuck will be able to handle the rest. She's going to stay at the ranch one week.''

"Good. That must take a load off your mind."

"It does. I don't know…" she began and the urge to cry suddenly reached up and grabbed her. Overwhelming feelings of melancholy, of grief, of her gratitude toward her sister, descended on her at once. She managed to hold back tears, but her voice cracked a little. "I d-don't know what I w-would have done without her d-during the h-hard times.''

The usual hard edge in Case's eyes softened a bit, and he said carefully, "Your sister wants to help you, Sarah. She loves you."

"I know. It's just that she's sacrificed so much already for me."

"Delaney wouldn't think of it that way."

Her sister had postponed their family vacation to Hawaii just to stay with her for the summer. She'd left her husband for weeks at a time, and disrupted her household. Sarah hated asking anything more of her. Being an independent soul and having lost her parents at a young age, Sarah had gone all through her adult life without depending on anyone. Except Reid. But that was different, she surmised because married people were supposed to help and support one another. Without Reid by her side, Sarah knew she'd be on her own. The grandmother who raised her and Delaney passed away three years ago.

If she had to, she'd face childbirth alone, too, but Delaney insisted she wanted to be a part of the baby's birth. She'd been enthusiastic about the delivery and so caring that Sarah would never be able to fully repay the favor, or show Delaney just how much her selfless help had meant to her.

"Delaney has been wonderful," she said, thinking aloud.

Sarah noticed that Case had stopped eating. Half a slice of pie still sat on his plate. Oh Lord, that's all she needed. *Make the man feel so sorry for you that he loses his gigantic appetite, Sarah.* "Your ice cream is melting, Case."

He grinned and lifted his spoon. "Never could take a teary-eyed woman."

"I'm not teary-eyed," she said with indignation. It was better to spar with Case than have him feel sorry for her. Sarah hated the moods that came hand in hand with pregnancy. Often she knew she was being irrational or just plain difficult, but she was powerless to stop it.

"Yes, ma'am."

A dollop of ice cream landed on his chin and stayed there. Without conscious thought, Sarah leaned over and wiped away the droplet with her finger. Case grabbed her finger gently and peered deep into her eyes, holding her hand to his chin. Temptation and danger cast a dark spark in his gaze. Sarah's heartbeats sped up just looking into those eyes. His touch did things to her, things she didn't want to encourage or entertain yet she'd certainly felt it and was powerless to slow the pace of her heart. "If you were any other woman," he said, letting her imagination take hold, "this might have gotten interesting."

Sarah knew all too well what happened when Case got "interested." For about five minutes in his life, she'd been the object of his desire on her prom night. That evening had been a disaster. Not only had Case tricked her but he'd also made Sarah doubt herself and her love for Reid. That had been a hard pill to swallow because of all the men in the world, Reid Jarrett deserved her love completely and unconditionally. He was a good man, solid and sure. Sarah had been enraged with Case and his hard-hearted game. He'd proven outright that he could never be trusted.

"But I'm not," she responded firmly, removing her hand from his chin, "any other woman."

She was his brother's pregnant widow and a woman who would always be wary of him. That about sized it up. She couldn't allow her bouts of loneliness to sway her resolve.

Eyes twinkling now, in direct contrast to the hot look he'd just given her, he had the good sense to back off. "No, ma'am. You're certainly not just any woman, Sarah." He lowered his voice. "I've always known that."

The soft way he said those words brought unexpected tingles and Sarah hid her smile. At eight months pregnant, Sarah wasn't used to hearing too many compliments.

She put her head down and toyed with her salad.

"Well hello, cowboy," a deep sultry voice called from across the room. Sarah snapped her head up to find Case frowning, then followed the line of his vision. Josie Miller, one of Case's old girlfriends, sauntered up to the table. The leggy redhead had eyes only for Case.

"Hello, Josie." Case seemed to eye her with typical male scrutiny.

"How've you been, Case. Long time, huh?"

"Yeah, I'd say it's been a long time." Case pushed his dish away and stretched out. "Just got back in town, actually. I took Sarah to her doctor's appointment today."

Sarah wanted to scream from the proprietary way Case had thrown that bit of information out. She'd just barely allowed him to accompany her to that appointment and

Case made it sound as if…as if they would be sharing more than her medical appointments.

Josie's wide smile faded, glancing from Case to her. "Oh, hello, Sarah. When's the baby due? You look like you're ready to pop."

"Babies don't pop, Josie," Case said, coming to Sarah's defense before she had a chance to respond. It more than irritated her that Case would be answering questions on her behalf.

"The baby's due in about one month, Josie."

"Oh, that so?" Josie swung her hip in Case's direction, but he didn't appear to notice.

"Yes," Sarah answered. "I can hardly wait."

Josie tossed her long red hair off her shoulder. "I bet. You plan on being the surrogate daddy, Case?" The woman seemed truly intent on his answer.

"Well, I, uh." Case blinked and fumbled with an answer. "Not exactly."

"My child will know who his father is, Josie. And that Case is his uncle." Sarah hoped she left no room for doubt.

"I see. Sure. The three of you all, living in that little ole ranch house together. Seems to me, that baby might get a teeny bit confused."

Heat surged up Sarah's throat and stung her face. She couldn't look at Case. She couldn't look at Josie. The woman hit the nail right on the head. Sarah had been thinking that very thing ever since Case showed up yesterday. She hadn't expected his arrival and now all sorts of doubts were filtering in about their living arrangements once the baby came.

She'd planned on keeping Reid's memory alive by speaking of him often and showing her child pictures of his father. But Case was the spitting image of Reid. With all three of them living under one roof, things could get confusing all the way around.

"I'm sure you folks will work it all out," Josie said smugly, then directed her attention back to Case, "but if you get at all tired of the family scene, Case, you have my number. Don't hesitate."

Case pursed his lips and nodded grimly. "'Night, Josie."

"Same to you all," she said sweetly.

"She's not subtle," Sarah said, once Josie returned to her table across the diner. Sarah decided to keep Josie's marital problems to herself having never been one to gossip. But the fact remained Josie had been married and divorced twice since high school.

Case chuckled, his tight face giving way to a smile. "She never was."

"You liked her once."

"I liked a lot of women, once." He let out a deep sigh. "Those days are long gone."

Sarah found that hard to believe. Case Jarrett with his devastating good looks and aloof attitude had been a heartbreaker. He liked women, all kinds of women and had always been the first to admit that. "You don't mean you plan on settling down, do you?"

That could solve her problem. If Case had a wife, then Sarah wouldn't feel so doggone awkward with him underfoot.

Case shook his head. "*Noooo. Settling down* means getting involved with a woman. I've just about sworn off females."

"I give you about a week, Case."

"I'm serious," he said, leaning forward. "I'm going to focus on the ranch and...uh—"

"And?" Case was holding something back. She could see it in his eyes and in the way his shoulders stiffened.

"Nothing, Sarah. You ready to go?"

"Yes. I'm all through."

"Let's get on back home," he said impatiently.

Sarah cringed inwardly at how Case used the very same expression Reid would whisper in her ear when he was impatient to get Sarah home. To make love. They'd spend a long sweet night together, loving.

How different her life was now.

There'd be no more nights of love and no more sweet embraces.

The only thing she had to look forward to was the arrival of the baby. That would be enough to see her through long lonely nights.

On the way home, Case pulled up to the Beckman Bridle Homes trailer located just outside of Prescott. The sign out front showed a planned community with a country club, golf course and boasted five hundred new "bridle path homes." Hell, every damn ranch within a twenty-mile radius was a bridle path home. And if the path wasn't there, you simply mounted your cow pony and etched one out of the land.

"Case, what are you doing here?" Sarah asked.

"I was thinking I'd go in there and give those land agents a piece of my mind."

"I don't think they'll come around again."

"Look at that sign, Sarah," he said, gesturing toward the large painted signpost. "Doesn't appear to me that they're going to give up. Looks as though they got this whole thing planned and nothing's going to stop them. I heard that five ranches have already agreed to their terms."

"Case, I can't say as I blame them. The smaller ranches haven't turned a profit in years. Those folks were just barely holding on. The offer came at a good time for them."

"And what about McPherson's barn? Don't folks care that these people they're selling to have no compunction?"

"I know it seems suspicious, Case, but we have no proof that Beckman Corporation had anything to do with that fire. Could have been an accident."

He scoffed at that. Case was certain that barn burned down because of foul play. He wasn't going to let anything like that happen at the Triple R. He doubted the corporation would buckle under just because one woman lifted a rifle and shooed their agent off the property. Brave as she was, Sarah just didn't have it in her to truly intimidate another living soul. That Merriman fella probably just decided to leave the pregnant woman be and find another approach.

"Besides, Case. It looks like they're closed for the day."

Case did a cursory glance and found Sarah to be right. Everything looked locked up good and tight as the small Closed sign on the far right window indicated.

"Yeah, guess you're right." Case would have to deal with them later. It was best Sarah not be around when he did. He wouldn't want her to get upset if things got ugly.

Case drove off slowly, noting Sarah putting her hand on her abdomen. "Everything okay?" he asked, peering at her from the corner of his eye.

A warm smile graced her face. "Yeah, just fine, Case. The baby is moving a whole lot."

Case swallowed a lump in his throat. He'd never been

the sentimental type, but seeing Sarah so at peace, enjoying the movements of that little babe, twisted something in his gut.

"He gets fidgety this time of night," Sarah said softly.

"Does it hurt, with him moving around like that?" Heck, it wasn't as if there was lots of room in there.

"No, doesn't hurt at all. Oh," she said sharply, then smiled, "but he's very active. I think he just kicked my ribs."

"And that doesn't hurt?"

"Well, it's a good kind of pain and doesn't last long."

Case nodded and returned his focus to the road. He had a lot to learn about babies. Tonight, he'd read through the brochure Dr. Michaels had given him.

They drove on in silence. Case noticed Sarah yawning several times. She'd had a long tiring day. He probably shouldn't have insisted they stop to eat, but sometimes he forgot that she needed more rest than usual.

The sun set on the horizon and it was dark by the time Case pulled up to the house. About fifteen minutes earlier, Sarah had fallen asleep, her head lodging uncomfortably against the truck's window. He hated to wake her, but darn it, she'd get a kink in her neck from the way she'd fallen asleep.

Quietly Case slid his body next to her. "Sarah," he whispered, "we're home."

Sarah didn't budge.

"Sarah," he repeated a little louder. He put his arm around her shoulder and gently shook her.

"Mmmm," she murmured and turned into his arms. Drugged by sleep, Sarah rested her head onto his chest and snuggled in. Golden strands of hair tickled his hand in a silken caress. Case sat there a moment, uncertain as to what to do. He listened to her deep breaths, taking in the flowery scent that was Sarah's alone.

"Sarah," he whispered again, but she didn't respond at all this time. The woman was definitely out.

Case folded his arm around her, holding her against him, letting her sleep. He forced himself to relax and lean back a little bit. Sarah flowed against him, but didn't stir.

She wouldn't like this, if she knew. But hell, Case had tried to wake her, several times. The woman was tired and needed her sleep. Case decided to enjoy this secret time with her. How long had he dreamt of holding her this way? Of taking her into his arms, and kissing her until kissing wasn't enough? He'd wanted Sarah for so long, he'd had to banish her from his thoughts at night so he could get some sleep. And now, he held her in his arms, as he'd always imagined.

Case wouldn't torture himself with those thoughts. He couldn't have Sarah. She had no use for him in her life. He'd made a promise to Reid to watch out for her and the baby. He'd lay down his life doing that, but Case knew that's all it would ever be. He couldn't compete with his brother's memory. For all he knew Sarah was still in love with Reid. At least that's the uneasy feeling he got every time she looked at him, as though she was disappointed that he wasn't Reid.

Maybe Sarah felt the wrong brother had been taken. Hell, Case rode around with that guilt, too. He was the one with the dangerous profession. Busting broncs nearly took out his eye and crushed his cheekbone, but ironically it was Reid who'd been injured in a nightmarish accident that eventually took his life. If Case had been here at the ranch, helping out, maybe Reid wouldn't have died.

In his heart Case believed Sarah would never look at

him and see him clearly, for the man he truly was. He'd let her believe him to be a scoundrel for so long she'd never have any other opinion of him. Perhaps it was better that way.

When Sarah flinched, Case peered sharply down at her belly. He could see ripples, a small tide of movement. His better sense gave way to desire. Case laid his hand carefully on Sarah's stomach. A little flutter, then a jolt met with his hand. The baby had spunk. Case stifled a chuckle, but a smile split his face wide open. No doubt, this child was a Jarrett.

A miracle lay under his fingertips. Case sat in wonder, holding the woman he wanted, feeling new life reach up and touch him. He closed his eyes and a deep sense of peace, of tranquillity, of something stronger he didn't dare name, washed over him. For a moment, he knew how Sarah must feel, carrying this child, nurturing it with all the love she had in her heart. Case brushed a soft kiss on Sarah's forehead.

And wished she'd sleep in his arms all night long.

# Three

Sarah sat in a lawn chair under a shady cottonwood tree in Bobbi Sue Curry's backyard and opened another gift. Her best friend had insisted on giving her a baby shower and so nearly all the female population of Barrel Springs was upon her. The women chattered and laughed happily as Sarah was presented with just about everything her new child would ever need. Her friends had been generous, even though she knew many were having their own financial difficulties, which made their generosity even more heartwarming.

"A car seat!" Sarah exclaimed, after opening the rather large rectangular box with the "help" of Bobbi Sue's five-year-old daughter, Maureen. "Now I'll have two. Thank you so much," she said, smiling at Amelia Velacruz, an old high school friend.

"You can return it for something else, Sarah. If you don't need two," Amelia promptly offered.

"She'll need 'em both, that's for sure," Judy Melcher, another of her old school friends called out. "Case will need one for his truck."

A rapid rise of heat flamed her cheeks. Sarah thought she must have blushed two shades of red. Ever since Case had moved back one week ago, she'd heard talk. Nothing much had been said directly to her, but there'd been plenty of innuendo about Case stepping in for his brother. Most of the comments seemed innocent enough, a way for folks to ease their curiosity about the goings-on at the Triple R, but Sarah had been hard-pressed as to how to clear things up exactly. Case was home, but he certainly wasn't "stepping" in for his brother.

At least not where she was concerned.

He was home to tend to the ranch. Finally he'd owned up to his responsibility, but Sarah doubted he'd stay on long. Case had a restless nature; he wasn't someone you could bank on for the long haul. Sarah knew this just as sure as she knew her baby had just knocked her in the ribs again. She smiled, thinking how rambunctious her child was…and how healthy.

Thank heavens for that.

"That baby will know how to ride a wild bronc before he walks, if Case has anything to say about it," one woman announced.

Sarah came out of her musings to respond. "Case won't," she said, perhaps too firmly as a hush stole over the ladies, "have anything to say about it."

Sarah noted her friends' faces, some staring with wide eyes, others averting their attention completely. What had gotten into them? She'd only stated a fact. Case Jarrett wouldn't have any say as to how she would raise her baby. Heavens, he'd only just come back to the ranch, and the entire town, practically, was making them into a couple. No. Everyone was trying to make them into a family. Sarah had learned the hard way that life didn't always fit into nicely wrapped packages complete with perfectly tied bows, like the remaining gifts on the table. No, life was more messy than that.

Just then, the back screen door slammed and Sarah turned around. Case stood at the opened doorway, staring at her. In that instant she knew he'd been there long enough to hear what she'd said. Dread mixed with misery as she peered into his eyes. She'd hurt him, yet there he stood, looking as handsome as ever and smiling at her. That smile always seemed to create butterfly flutters in her stomach. "Case, w-what are you doing here?"

Bobbi Sue handed him a plate filled with food and a glass of iced tea. "I thought I'd save Bobbi Sue and Carl a trip and pick you up myself. I brought my truck to haul all the gifts back to the ranch."

"Oh," she said, slumping a bit in her chair, "that's very thoughtful."

"I thought so, too," Bobbi Sue said then pointed to a seat on the porch in the shade. "Take a load off, Case. Sarah's about through, just a few more gifts to open then we'll have cake. Won't be but another half an hour."

Case planted himself down with plate in hand. "Don't mind if I do," he said, thanking Bobbi Sue, then winking at Sarah. "You go on and finish up, darlin'. I'll wait."

Sarah was handed the next gift, a pretty pink and blue basket. She glanced into the crowd of her friends and smiled tentatively. They seemed to have one eye on Case and the other on her, waiting and watching. For what exactly, Sarah didn't know but so many of her friends were nodding approval or casting her undisguised smirks.

One hour later, Sarah gave Bobbi Sue a big hug. "Thanks so much," she said, stepping out onto the front steps. "I don't think the baby will be wanting for a thing now."

"Nope, I don't think so. I'm glad the shower was such a success. You deserve every good thing that comes along, Sarah."

Sarah sighed and patted her belly. "The baby is all I need now, Bobbi Sue. It'll be the best thing that comes along in my lifetime."

Bobbi Sue looked out onto the front yard, where Carl was helping Case load the gifts up into the bed of his truck. "There's nothing like a child, Sarah, that's true. My little Maureen has brought us nothing but joy, even if she's still resisting going to school every day. But honey, don't sell yourself short. You've got a whole lot of living yet to do. And looks to me, there's more than just one good thing in store for you in this life."

Sarah directed her gaze to Case. Bobbi Sue couldn't possibly mean...no, she wouldn't even entertain such thoughts. "You're not talking about Case, are you?"

"He might be just what you need, Sarah. I had a crush on him in high school. Did I ever tell you that?"

Sarah chuckled. "You and about every other starry-eyed female. I think he made the rounds with almost all of them."

"Ah, I don't think it was all that many, Sarah. Surely I wasn't so lucky."

"Consider it a blessing, Bobbi Sue. Case broke more hearts than a dog's got fleas."

"Did he ever break your heart, Sarah?"

Sarah's eyes went wide. "Bobbi Sue, you know better. Case and I weren't ever friends, much less anything else." Sarah tried to block out the image of Case, dressed in an elegant black suit, coming to her door on prom night and kissing her senseless. They'd done more than kiss and Sarah still recalled the exquisite sensations Case had aroused in her that night. She trembled at the thought. Case had made her feel things she'd never experienced before. He'd shown her a side of passion, of heat and desire that she'd never known. He'd had no right, yet the memory of being with him, had often haunted her. Sarah couldn't allow her mind to travel that path. She couldn't forget the terrible trick he'd played on her. She couldn't forget that he was Reid's brother, either.

Bobbi Sue shook her head and sighed dramatically. Her best friend could outshine any Hollywood type with her acting ability. "He's still a good-looking son of a gun, isn't he?"

Sarah couldn't deny that. The Jarrett twins were tall, dark and handsome. But there were differences between Case and Reid—huge differences—and Sarah wondered again how she'd ever mistaken Case for Reid all those years ago.

"He won't be around long, Bobbi Sue. I just have a feeling he'll get tired of the ranch and take off again."

Bobbi Sue shook her head. "I don't think so, Sarah. I think you've got to give Case more credit than that. Give him a chance to prove himself. This time he's got that 'I'm where I belong' look about him. I notice it every time the man looks your way."

Sarah laughed at Bobbi Sue's obvious attempt to stir up something that wouldn't even budge in the pot. And she didn't think she could give Case another chance. She'd done that so often in the past because he was Reid's brother. All he'd managed to do was disappoint her, time and again. "I'll try," she said to appease her friend, hoping that she could one day work past her resentment of him.

"Good. Well, looks like the men have packed all up."

Sarah glanced at the truck. Case was leaning up against it casually, one arm slung along the side of the fully loaded bed, speaking with Carl. He straightened up immediately when he saw her.

"You ready?" he asked. "Because I think you've got enough stuff in here to fill up two nurseries."

Carl chuckled. "I offered to ride up to the ranch to help unload, but Case didn't want my help."

"Naw, you got a wife to keep happy right here. And little Mo tells me, she's got a new bike for you to put together tonight."

"That's right," Bobbi Sue called out, "you don't want to disappoint your daughter now, do you?"

Carl shrugged then shook Case's hand, thanking him for the help. Sarah went down the steps slowly then hugged Carl and Bobbi Sue one last time. "I love you both. Thanks for a wonderful day," she said, tears once again misting up her eyes.

"Case, take this woman home before I start bawling myself," Bobbi Sue said with a smile.

Case helped Sarah up into the truck and waved goodbye. He drove slowly as they made their way onto the road leading to the ranch. Sarah fought to keep her eyes open. It had been a long, wonderful, *exhausting* day but the last thing she wanted to do, was to fall asleep in Case's truck again.

Waking up, all cozy and warm in Case's arms that night had really thrown her. Before opening her eyes, she remembered feeling so peaceful. So sheltered and safe. She'd been wrapped tight in a cocoon of heat, his male scent drifting up and encasing her in comfort. She'd stayed there a moment, working through her confusion, but once she realized through a thin layer of hazy awareness that she'd cuddled up with Case she nearly bolted out the truck's door. Case stopped her, fearing that she'd fall out and get injured. She blushed down to her toes when he told her she'd been sleeping in his arms for three hours. *Three hours.* He claimed he'd tried and tried to wake her, but finally gave up thinking she needed her sleep more than anything else at that moment.

"Where do you want all the gifts to go?" Case asked, turning his attention to her.

"Most of them go into the baby nursery. Some of the bigger pieces have to be assembled. I'd like to get the crib put up as soon as possible. I don't know why, but I'm getting a little antsy."

"I'll do it tonight, if you want," he offered.

"I was going to give it a try," she said lamely, trying not to sound too stubborn. "But you can help, if you have the time."

"I'll help you after supper, Sarah," he said, looking into her eyes. "I have to check up on things by Red Ridge this afternoon after I unload. There's a few hours of daylight left."

"That's fine with me, Case. I'll have supper ready by seven."

"Okay. We'll tackle the crib and playpen after we eat."

She felt a renewed sense of excitement now, just thinking of the baby in the finished nursery.


Sarah glanced at the beef stew sitting on the table, getting cold. She expected Case to come barreling through the door any minute now, chock full of excuses. It was a good half an hour past the time he'd assured her he'd be home for supper.

She was tired and hungry and getting angrier by the minute. She'd tried calling him on his cell phone and got nothing. It wasn't unusual for the phone not to work clear up by Red Ridge where Case claimed he was heading. That mountain location had always been the phone company's black hole area, a spot so remote they couldn't ever seem to get service.

"Just sit yourself down, Sarah, and eat," she muttered. She sat down and ladled a portion of stew onto her plate. She brought the spoon to her mouth ready to take her first bite then lowered it back down. "Darn it, Case," she griped, tamping down her anger and replacing it with worry. Case wasn't trustworthy, she reminded herself. She shouldn't be overly concerned. Perhaps something better had presented itself to Case, like a female ready to give him a good time.

But in the back of her mind, Sarah felt something was amiss. Intuition told her Case might be in trouble. There had been those disguised threats by the land agents. And what if McPherson's barn burning down hadn't been an accident? What if Jarrett land was next on the list?

Sarah jumped up and grabbed her car keys. Leaving the meal sitting on the table, she locked up the house and got into her Explorer. Crimson Arizona dust spiraled up as she headed off in the direction of Red Ridge in a hurry.

Sarah drove deep in the canyon, keeping a steady look out for Case. He'd be on horseback she surmised, since his black pickup had been outside the house, right where he'd left it when he'd unloaded her shower gifts. "He's probably all right," she mumbled urgently, her temper rising at his thoughtlessness putting her through this worry. "He better be all right."

The mountain was awash in color. Rock formations shooting up toward the clouds in brilliant hues of oranges and reds cast a fiery glow to the barren canyon. Sarah had always loved Red Ridge for its towering magnificence. The land here humbled a person, awing them with the majesty of nature.

Ten minutes later, she spotted a dark speck off in the distance. She drove forward cautiously until she'd assured herself it was Case. He wasn't mounted. Diamond, his favorite gray mare ambled several paces behind.

Sarah stopped the car a few yards away, the land being too jutted for her to attempt in her pregnant state. The bumpy ride had already caused an ache in her side. She ignored the pain and slowly climbed down from the seat to walk over to Case.

"Sarah," he said, his eyes blurring. "W-what are you doing here?"

Sarah gasped when she noticed blood running down the side of Case's face and dripping onto the darkness of his shirt. "Case, what happened to you?" Moving closer, Sarah saw a knot alongside his head. She reached up and gently moved aside a few locks of hair to get a better look. "Oh, that's a nasty bump." She fingered the bump tentatively. "Are you hurting?"

"Just my pride, darlin'." He cocked his head then flinched from the sudden movement. Taking out a bandanna from his back pocket, he dabbed at the blood on his face. Sarah stepped back to look into his eyes. He focused on her, but it seemed to take a bit of doing. "You shouldn't have come way out here."

"It's Saturday night, Case. All the hands have gone home for the weekend and someone had to come check on you. Tell me what happened?"

Case ran his hand down the side of his face that hadn't been bloodied. "A big old grouchy hawk swooped down on us and spooked Diamond. She reared back and bucked. The mare caught me off guard. Next thing I know, I'm flying through the air. Landed my head on a hard rock. I think I was out for a few minutes.''

Sarah didn't like the way Case was swaying as he spoke. His eyes looked glassy. He had trouble focusing. "I'm afraid you might have been out longer than you think. It's nearly dark. You were supposed to be home an hour ago. You might have a concussion, Case."

"Naw. I've had my share of those, Sarah. I know the feeling. Mostly my ego is damaged. I've ridden bucking broncos all my adult life. Getting caught by a spooked mare, now that's a hard one to swallow."

"Still, you should see a doctor."

"Nope. Just a hot bath will do. I'll be fine." The corners of his mouth lifted in a smile, but the sudden motion cost him. He winced in pain.

Sarah felt a sudden tightening in her abdomen. She gripped her stomach. A steady stream of water gushed out, running down her legs. "Oh, no," she cried out, doubling over.

"What? Sarah, what's wrong?"

The pain intensified. "I think...oh," she exclaimed, the pain gripping her tight. "I think...the baby's coming," she managed to say.

"Now?" Case's shaky voice filled her with fear. "But you have weeks to go," he said in disbelief.

On instinct, Sarah knew the baby was coming early. This was no false alarm. And she knew the circumstances. They were out in a desolate part of the range, with no form of communication. Case probably had a concussion. And it appeared from the intensity of her contractions that the baby wasn't going to wait.

When the pain subsided, Sarah glanced up. Case's face had gone pale. "Now. Babies don't always come on schedule."

Case straightened and nodded, a determined light coming into his eyes. "Okay, okay. Let's get you into the car. We'll make it to the hospital in half an hour."

"Okay," Sarah said numbly and walked slowly to the car with Case's arm around her shoulder. He helped her up, carefully. Another contraction hit hard. Her stomach tightened and cramped. She tried to remember to breathe. Relax. Take a deep abdominal breath. Let the muscles go loose and limp. She reminded herself of her childbirth training. *"Ohhhh!"*

"Sarah?" Case brushed her hair from her face. "Sarah, what can I do?"

"I, uh, just drive, Case. And hurry."

"You got it."

Case got into the car and started the motor. He took it slow on the road, but Sarah felt every pit, every jut. When another hard contraction hit, Sarah screamed. "Stop!"

Case slammed on the brakes.

She doubled over again and tried to breathe slowly, taking calming breaths. "They're so p-powerful," she said, gasping when the contraction reached its peak.

Case grabbed for the car phone. "I'm calling for help."

Sarah didn't have the strength to tell him the phone wouldn't work. He'd find out soon enough.

Case cursed up a storm then slammed the phone back into its socket. "Damn it, I can't get through." He lifted her chin and looked into her eyes. "Sarah, I've gotta get you to the hospital."

She nodded and he started the motor up.

Just then, another powerful contraction hit. *"Ohhhh."* This wasn't the way it was supposed to happen. Sarah recalled her childbirth instructor saying most first-time babies take their time. Often, the contractions come twenty minutes apart. Hers seemed to be hitting every two minutes.

She could see Case's eyes half on her, half on the road. "I'm sorry, honey. If there was anything I could do, I'd do it."

They hit a large bump in the road. It was dark out now. Case tried to find the best route out of the canyon, but Sarah was becoming increasingly more uncomfortable. "Case, you have to stop."

Case slowed the car and peered at her. "I *have* to get you to the hospital."

Sarah shook her head and grabbed on to his sleeve. "No, Case. There isn't time. The baby's coming too fast."

Case stopped the car again and stared at her, blinking several times. She met the fear in his eyes with her own. There was no way around this, no help for it. Sarah knew what he had to do. The contractions were intense and coming far too frequently. She pleaded with him now. He was her only hope. "Case, you have to deliver my baby."

# Four

Case Jarrett swore silently, but wouldn't let Sarah see his apprehension. He'd scanned over the literature Dr. Michaels had given him, but had never once thought he'd be called upon to deliver Sarah's baby. Yet, he had no other option. And as Sarah let out another plea when a contraction hit, Case calmed her. "Okay, Sarah. We're going to do this together. Don't you worry, darlin'. I'm here and I won't let you down."

Sarah's eyes met his, searching. He nodded, keeping her locked in his gaze until her fear slowly dissipated. She was counting on him, he knew, and Case had to muster all of his courage to help her.

Lord help him if anything went wrong.

Case cast her a quick reassuring smile. "I'm going to get you more comfortable, for one." He opened the trunk, found an old but clean Navajo blanket and pulled out a flashlight as well.

With the lights on in the car, Case helped Sarah into the back seat. She removed her pants and covered up modestly with the blanket he'd given her.

Another contraction hit and Sarah moaned. Her restraint and the effort she made to stay in control was apparent on her face as she took deep calming breaths. Case grasped hold of her hand and stroked her gently. "That's good, sweetheart. Breathe in and out slowly."

She squeezed his hand tight. "I th-think the baby is m-moving down. I can f-feel it, Case." Sarah began to shake, her body reacting to the intensity of the contractions. "Transition," she moaned. "W-won't be l-long now before I s-start pushing." With wide eyes, Sarah gauged his expression.

A master of cool, Case smiled again and although he'd broken out in a sweat, he knew Sarah was far too busy to notice. Bending over, he brushed aside a few strands of hair that had fallen into her eyes. He spoke softly, meeting her eyes again, with a calmness he didn't really feel. "That's good. The baby's coming real soon."

Case knew a hundred things could go wrong, but he banked on Sarah's strength, her determination and her love for the baby to put them both on the right path. He gave her hand a little squeeze. "You're doing great, Sarah."

She nodded, looking deep into his eyes and took another deep breath.

"Let it out, darlin'. Breathe in and out real slow. That's good," Case said, beginning to gain a bit of confidence. He'd pushed his hazy mind to the limit, but he had recalled some of the things a coach needed to do in order to help. Thanks to Dr. Michaels and her little brochure.

"I have to push!" Sarah said urgently.

Case helped Sarah get into place and as awkward as it was in the back seat of the car, they managed to get her into somewhat of a pushing position. "Okay?" he asked.

Sarah nodded and took a breath.

"I'm here for you, Sarah. Don't you worry about a thing. Jarretts are strong. This baby is coming out, no trouble at all."

She met his eyes again as if connecting with him gave her strength. Case hoped so, they both needed to be strong right now. When she pushed hard, her face contorted, but not so much with pain as sheer resolve, he noted. Case held her, whispered encouraging words in her ear, helped her with one contraction after another and realized that each guttural sound she made brought the baby that much closer to the birth. "You're doing real good, sweetheart," he said, holding her close. "Won't be long now."

Ten minutes later, with one last final push, the new baby Jarrett was born. Case caught her as she entered the world and was struck immediately by the wonder of it all.

Case held the child in his arms, a wiggling, wet, little bundle that didn't look much like a baby at all. Yet, she was beautiful all the same. She was his niece, the child he helped bring into the world. Nothing he'd ever done in the past, meant as much, or had had this profound an effect on him. Awed into silence from the miracle that he'd just witnessed, Case could only hold her carefully for a moment, staring into eyes barely struggling to open. The baby cried, little soft sounds that were heaven to Case's ears. The child was healthy and apparently, no worse for wear. "Here she is," he said softly, handing Sarah her child. "It's a girl."

Tears of joy streamed down Sarah's face, a look of

pure love shining in her eyes. "Oh, she's beautiful." She took hold of the baby's hand. "Hello, little Christiana."

Case grabbed the blanket and wrapped the baby, wiping her dry in places, covering both mother and child. The baby found her mother's breast easily and began suckling. "She is that," Case said, nearly tongue-tied watching the scene, then he focused on the woman who had just given birth. "You feeling all right, Sarah?"

"I think so," she said, smiling down at her baby. "We did all right, didn't we?"

"Just fine, darlin'. Any fainting I plan to do will be in private." He winked and smiled but Sarah didn't smile back. Instead, she grasped his hand in hers and held on tight. Her blue eyes softened and filled with gratitude. She spoke quietly, "I'll never forget what you did, Case. You delivered my baby."

Case sighed, his chest heavy with emotion. "Ah, Sarah. Don't think I'll ever forget, either." He peered down at the babe and raw powerful feelings welled up, shocking him to his bones at how such a small little life, a new being, could impact him so fully. "Now, are you ready for a drive? I've got to get you two to the hospital. Once we're out of the canyon, I'll phone ahead. You'll be taken care of properlike."

Sarah leaned back and sighed, a look of total and complete contentment on her face as she peered at her baby. Sarah Johnston Jarrett was a woman made for mothering. "We're ready, Case," she said softly, the baby nuzzling at her breast. "But we've already been taken care of properlike."

Christiana Marie Jarrett weighed in at five pounds three ounces, born four weeks early. For the two days Sarah had been in the hospital, Case had divided his time between working the ranch, visiting Sarah and his new baby niece and building a rocking horse for her.

Case insisted on picking Sarah up from the hospital and once they reached the Triple R, he helped her out of the car. "You're home," he said to Sarah, then bent into the back seat and lifted Christiana out of her car seat. "And so are you, little one. Welcome to the Triple R, Christie."

Christiana squawked, bringing a look of concern to Sarah's face. Case handed the baby over to her. "She's fine, darlin'. Just testing out her lungs."

Sarah laughed, carefully holding her child in her arms. Pete and several of the ranch hands walked over, anxious to catch a glimpse of the new arrival.

"*Ahhh,* she's a pretty one, just like her mama," Pete said, keeping a safe distance away. Babies seemed to make most men real nervous.

"Thanks, Pete," Sarah said, lifting the baby up a bit so that all the men could see her. "Say hello to everyone, Christiana." Sarah and the baby were greeted with cheers of congratulations and good wishes.

Case put a hand to Sarah's back to brace her, but also to renew the connection they'd shared when they'd delivered the baby together. It felt right touching Sarah, keeping both mother and baby safe. An uncanny sense of pride swelled within Case's chest. "I think mama and baby need to get some rest now." Lines of fatigue had appeared on Sarah's joyous face. Case knew Sarah was tired. "Let's get you inside the house."

Sarah nodded, waving goodbye to everyone. Case kept a hand to her back, guiding her up the stairs. "I finished setting up the nursery," he said, "but I'm not sure you're gonna like where I put things."

"Case, you've done so much already," Sarah said, her voice laced with gratitude. "I'm sure it'll be just fine."

When Sarah entered the baby's nursery, a look of admiration stole over her face as she held back tears. "Oh, it's lovely." Case hadn't been sure where to put the crib, diaper changer and dresser, but he'd arranged the furniture the best that he could. An oak rocking chair sat in one corner of the room and the rocking horse he'd made for the baby, he'd placed on the other side.

Sarah walked over to the rocking horse. "Did you make this?"

With a slow nod, Case replied, "Will be a while before she's able to ride it, but it's fitting, don't you think? Christiana needs to learn how to ride a horse. I figured this one first, before she gets on the real thing."

Sarah drew in her bottom lip, her voice unsteady. "She'll love it. Thank you, Case."

"You're welcome." Case let out a breath. "I'll get your bags from the car. You'll be wanting to move upstairs now, so you can be closer to the baby's room. Want me to take your room downstairs?"

"Oh? I hadn't thought about that. No need for you to move on our account. You're settled in up here. Unless, you think the crying will keep you from sleep?"

"Nothing keeps me from sleep, darlin'." Case grinned. "I'll get to it right away. You okay up here with the baby?"

"We'll be just fine. I think I'll rock her for a while." With care, Sarah handed the baby to Case then lowered herself down. Once she settled, Case kissed the baby on the forehead and handed her back to Sarah.

"Enjoy the ride," he said. "I'll get Pete and we'll have you moved upstairs real quick."

Sarah smiled, but her focus, her full attention was on

her baby. Case was nearly out the door, when Sarah called his name. "Case."

He turned to glance at her.

Sarah shook her head slightly, her eyes misting up. She said with sweet regard, "I don't know how to thank you for all you've done."

"I'm glad to do it, Sarah," he offered, leaving her with the baby. He'd do just about anything for Sarah and her baby, though the one thing he really wanted from Sarah, he could never have.

He had a promise to keep, and he sincerely doubted his brother Reid would approve of the images flashing in his head right now, of how Sarah could thank him properly.

Hell, there was nothing "proper" about it.

He wanted Sarah Johnston Jarrett in his bed and in his life. Keeping his distance would test his willpower to its limit.

Later that night, Sarah set Christiana in her crib, both mother and daughter quite exhausted. Christiana's bright blue eyes shuddered closed, surrendering the battle of sleep. Sarah covered her with a pretty pink blanket. "Sleep well, sweetheart. I'm right next door."

Even that distance seemed too far for Sarah. The baby had been alongside of her for two full days while in the hospital. Mother and daughter had yet to be separated. Reluctantly Sarah tiptoed out of the room, desperately fighting off the temptation to return.

Sarah stepped into the room adjacent to the nursery. It had once been the bedroom she'd shared with Reid. She had no choice but to have her things moved up here again. She wouldn't upend Case. The room down the hall had always been his. As children, Case and Reid had shared that room together. Yet, to be as near her baby as possible, Sarah took the master bedroom again, but it wasn't the same. One essential person was missing and he'd never be back. He'd never know his beautiful daughter or witness her growth, her first smile, her first step.

Sarah sighed and fought off the melancholy mood threatening to seize her. She'd decided long ago that she wouldn't dwell in the past, but live for the future. She'd loved Reid Jarrett with all of her heart, but he was gone now, and Sarah had a sweet little child to raise and a ranch to run.

Sarah slipped out of her maternity dress and put on her nightgown, a bout of fatigue finally hitting her. It had been an eventful day, coming home from the hospital, moving back into her bedroom, realizing that she'd be living with Case Jarrett, for as long as he decided to stay on.

Somehow, it seemed different now, with Christiana here and the three of them sharing the same home, each one to their own rooms. Case was family. He was Christiana's uncle, the man who had brought her into the world, yet Sarah still couldn't help or deny the wariness she felt around him.

He'd always made her nervous. She'd never trusted him.

The knock to her door startled her. She jumped out of bed and reached for her robe. "Just a minute," she called out, jamming her arms into the sleeves and tying up the belt.

She opened her door to find Case standing there, dressed in clean clothes and wearing his going-out Stetson. His dark-eyed perusal made her jittery and uninvited flutters invaded her insides. "Sorry, Sarah. Didn't think you'd get to bed so early. I should've guessed. You had a long day.''

"It's all right. Christiana's sleeping, so I thought I'd lay down for a spell."

"Good idea. You should rest, darlin'. I peeked in on little Christie just a minute ago." Case smiled, a quick flash of white teeth and Jarrett charm. "She sure is cute."

Sarah smiled, too, the mention of her baby bringing giddy motherly pride. "She sure is."

"Well, just wanted to see if you needed anything. I'm heading to town tonight. Can I pick anything up for you?"

Surprised, Sarah asked, "Are you going shopping?"

Case took a moment to answer, then shook his head. "Nope, but I'll stop at the store if you need anything."

"Oh, um, no. I think I have everything I need. Thanks for the offer, though."

"No problem. I won't be late. Should only be gone a few hours. You sure you're okay with me leaving?"

"Of course, Case. I told you, the baby and I aren't your responsibility. You go on. Have a fun time."

A puzzled look crossed his face. Case's brows arched. "Fun?"

Sarah amended her comment. She didn't want to pry. It was none of her business where Case was going this evening looking as handsome as the devil. Freshly groomed, wearing a crisp white shirt under a black suede vest, Case sure looked as though he was out for a night on the town. "Wherever you're going, have a nice time."

Case tipped his hat. "Good night, Sarah. See you in the morning."

"Good night," she said, closing her door.

And Sarah wondered if Case Jarrett would even come home this evening. Funny thing, an odd sensation stole over her when he said he was going out. She figured it was surprise more than anything else. It wasn't as though she'd expected any better from him, but it *was* her first night home with the baby.

"He couldn't even stick around one night," she whispered behind the door.

She'd always be beholden to him for delivering her baby, but she sure as anything knew, charm or no charm, Case Jarrett wasn't a man she could count on.

She hoped she'd never forget that.

# Five

"What do you think, Christiana? Think your mama can fit back into her jeans?" Sarah smiled at her baby propped up in the infant seat on the floor in her bedroom. The baby paid her no mind. She was far too interested in her own reflection, as she peered into the mirrored closet door.

Sarah tugged on her blue jeans, and although they fit more snugly than she liked, they were far better than her maternity clothes. Nine months, or rather eight in Sarah's case, was too long to subject a woman to the unfashionable garments made for pregnancy. "There," she said, gazing at her daughter in the mirror, "two weeks and three days, is all it took."

Sarah slipped on a tank top, the late September heat too stifling for anything else. They'd had a wave of hot weather lately, not too unusual for Arizona in early fall and Sarah usually didn't mind, but lately she'd been...overheated. She blamed it on mixed-up hormones, something having to do with the birth of Christiana and the next time she spoke with Dr. Michaels, she'd ask her about it. "Or it could be these tight jeans," she said with a self-conscious laugh. "Maybe I should have waited another week," she confided to the baby. Oblivious, Christiana closed her eyes.

Sarah kissed her softly on the forehead. She couldn't imagine putting on any more maternity clothes, so she grabbed her daughter's infant seat and headed down the stairs, tight jeans, heated body and all.

When she reached the kitchen, Case was already sitting at the table, with head down, poring over a batch of accounts. He didn't notice her and she wouldn't disturb his concentration. She set the infant seat down in the center of the table, making sure the baby was safe then turned to start breakfast.

"I made coffee," he said, his gaze still focused on the billing statements.

"Thanks." Sarah poured herself a cup of decaf, grateful that Case had been thoughtful enough to remember that while breast-feeding, she had to stay away from caffeine.

She heated up a skillet, took out cereal bowls and grabbed eggs out of the refrigerator. When she heard Case's soft voice, she turned, wondering what he'd said. She realized he hadn't been speaking to her but playing with Christiana. With a small noisy rattle, Case tried to get her attention. Sarah watched Case make silly faces, his expression soft, his dark, normally brooding eyes, even softer.

A wave of intense heat shot through her. Sarah blinked back her surprise at the sensations she experienced whenever Case was around. Once again she wondered about her mixed-up hormones. Boy, she'd better speak with Dr. Michaels real quick, she thought, as she turned to crack the eggs into the sizzling skillet.

"How many eggs would you like?" she asked, after she'd recovered from the bout of heat.

"Three," he answered, fully absorbed in his games with the baby.

Sarah didn't mind being ignored. She sort of liked the space Case had given her. He'd left her pretty much to her own devices. He'd been diligent working the ranch, doing chores and conferring with their foreman Pete on matters that Sarah didn't have time for now. In her mind, they were merely two people, sharing an interest in the ranch, who happened to be living under the same roof. This situation might just work out after all.

Sarah poured two cups of coffee and walked over to the table, setting one down in front of Case. "Here you go."

"Thanks, darlin'," Case said, finally lifting his head to glance at her, then all softness left his face and his mouth dropped open briefly. He took a hard swallow and his gaze took a quick detour from her face to the other pertinent parts of her anatomy. That doggone heat again, rose up her neck and burned her cheeks. Darn it! She knew she should have waited another week before stuffing herself into these jeans.

Case blew out a breath and stood, pinning her with a look so hot it rivaled the sizzling griddle she'd just turned on. "C-Case?" Her insides trembled. She prayed for nonchalance as she tilted her head and met his gaze head-on.

He cleared his throat, his eyes wide, raking her over, taking her in. "Damn, Sarah," he managed, then settled his gaze on her chest. Awareness Sarah hadn't experienced in months, coursed throughout her body in a way only definite male appreciation could promptly elicit. Suddenly she realized just how very revealing her tank top was, her breasts stretching the knit top to its limit. She hadn't thought much of it when she'd put it on. She'd only wanted to stay cool. Since breast-feeding Christiana, Sarah enjoyed a healthier cup size, but that Case had noticed her body taking shape again brought myriad sensations along with it.

He brought his body close enough for her to take in the scent of lime aftershave and fresh soap. Hot steam filled the air and she wasn't entirely sure it was created solely from the mugs of coffee.

Rooted to the spot, she couldn't pretend she didn't know what Case was thinking when he stared at her lips. Those deep dark penetrating eyes gave him away. Foolishly the wholly female, feminine part of her rejoiced. It was as dangerous as it was insane when Sarah stared back, noting the hard line of his jaw, the contours of his mouth.

He's Reid's brother, she warned herself.

She shouldn't be having these thoughts.

She shouldn't be feeling these feelings.

Yet, impending heat swamped her, creating awkward, uninvited quivers. It had been ages since she felt anything remotely like this. Ages, since she'd felt desirable. Case made her feel that way. He made her feel like she was the only woman on the planet right now. Sarah didn't have a response for Case. She couldn't come up with a word. He had started this and he was going to finish it.

He bent his head and Sarah told herself to run, to step away from this dangerous game, but instead she stood her ground, her heart racing like crazy. His lips burned hers with gentle heat when they touched. Wild, glorious sensations whirled within, causing havoc to her resolve. She remembered his kiss from one other night, long ago and the familiar, yet forbidden impact shattered her defenses. She made a tiny sound, one that had him pulling her against him. Their bodies meshed with heat, his, granite hard, hers, soft and pliant. He held her now, kissing her deeply and she returned his passion, unmindful of the consequences. Case had always been able to do that to her, make her forget things she'd be better off not forgetting.

But all too suddenly, her mind did clear and she realized what had just happened—she'd kissed Reid's brother. Guilt assailed her instantly and she broke off the kiss, stepping back and heaving a deep breath of air. Sarah admonished herself for allowing that kiss to happen.

Case's gaze rested on her with no apology. "I thought you beautiful when you were pregnant, but now…" Case stated with sincerity then let that thought linger as he turned away, flipping his account book closed. She heard him mumble almost beneath his breath, "It's gonna be murder living here with you."

He was out the door before she could respond. Not that she had a response. Her lips still burned from his kiss and her mind had pretty much turned to gooey oatmeal.

When the baby complained, a small squawk of boredom, Sarah was grateful for the distraction. She slumped down in the kitchen chair and stared into the light blue eyes of her beautiful daughter. She whispered, "Murder or not, Case Jarrett, we can't ever do that again."

Case mounted Diamond and with a wave to Pete, rode his horse deep into Jarrett grazing land. He had fences to check, a routine assessment that would take up most of the day. Hot sun burned across his face, his sunglasses and hat doing little to shield him from the grilling. But Case was damn glad he had a day's work ahead of him, away from the house.

He'd been struck like lightning, seeing Sarah waltz into the kitchen this morning, looking hotter than nature's force glaring down on him right now.

Damn. Sweet, wholesome, pretty-as-a-picture Sarah looked *hot* in those jeans, ponytail and all. How quickly her body had taken shape again. Motherhood did things to a woman's figure. Nice, sexy, appealing things that drove men wild.

Sarah did that to him. She drove him wild. And that kiss had nearly knocked him to his knees. Damn her. There was something special about Sarah that he hadn't found in any other woman. Something he wanted, bad. He shouldn't have kissed her, but she'd taken him completely by surprise this morning and Case couldn't keep his hands off.

An entire herd of stampeding cattle couldn't have stopped him from kissing her.

He groaned aloud, a deep guttural sound of pain. There wasn't a soul around to hear him anyway. "Ain't ever gonna happen, Jarrett."

And Case knew that for a fact. He hadn't come back to the ranch to seduce his brother's widow. He'd come back for far more noble a purpose, although, at times, Case thought he'd love to chuck his good intentions and claim Sarah for his own. "She ain't yours for the taking," he reminded himself, once again.

Taking care of the Triple R and keeping Sarah and the baby safe was his number one priority. If he could do that, then he figured he'd be square with Reid, once and for all. There was no backing down and no turning away. Not this time. He was here for as long as it took, forever, if need be. But Sarah wasn't included in the vow he'd made with his brother. And she certainly wasn't included in the unspoken bargain he'd made with himself.

Now all Case had to do was figure out a way he could live with Sarah underfoot and keep the ache out of his heart, his gut and his groin. Damn, the woman did things to his mind, too.

Case made it halfway into the property before he noticed a fence down. He dismounted Diamond and walked over to a post. With gloved hands, he attempted to lift it up, taking care not to tangle with the barbed wire. But the dang thing wouldn't come up. And as his gaze finally roved down the rest of the line, he noticed at least twenty yards of fence down. At least.

"Sonofabitch."

No wonder he couldn't lift the post—each section weighed down the others in a domino effect. He'd need his entire crew to come out here to right this.

Case knew this was no act of nature. They hadn't had a windstorm or a dust storm lately. The earth hadn't quaked fiercely, pulling down his fences. This was sabotage, pure and simple. And he'd be damned if he didn't know who was behind this.

Fury seeped in. Case swore violently then mounted Diamond again. No telling when this occurred, but his first thought was for Sarah and the baby. He'd check on them, then see to fixing his property.

"Sarah, Sarah!" Case called out, twenty minutes later. He'd stormed into the kitchen, but there was no sign of her. Impatiently, he strode through the rooms downstairs, then ascended the stairs, his pulse racing. "Sarah!"

With a shove, he pushed open the nursery door. "Sarah!"

"Shh," she whispered, but it was too late. Startled, Christiana pulled away from her mother's breast on the rocking chair and let out a humdinger of a wail.

Case stood rooted to the spot, satisfied that Sarah and the baby were all right, but half sick that he'd barged in and upset both mother and daughter.

"What is it?" Sarah said, her voice verging on anger as she rapidly adjusted her tank top.

"Sorry," he said, watching Sarah struggle now with a baby intent on having all of Barrel Springs hear her cries. "I had to make sure you were okay."

"Why? What's happened?"

Case couldn't hear himself think with Christiana screaming. "Here, give her to me," he said, putting out his arms, hoping Sarah wouldn't refuse.

She didn't. She handed her up to him, then bounded from the rocking chair. Case snuggled the baby in his arms, cradling her to his chest. He spoke softly, "Don't cry, Christie. Uncle Case has you now. Shh, pretty baby, don't you cry anymore."

To his relief and Sarah's astonishment, Christiana took a few gulps of air then stopped her sobbing. Case rocked her in his arms, swaying back and forth. "That's a good girl. Go on back to sleep."

"Case?" With hands planted on her hips, Sarah heaved a deep sigh, her chest rising up then falling.

Case blinked, his heart hammered, remembering his reaction to Sarah this morning and the powerful kiss they'd shared. Hell, he'd like to take Sarah in his arms and kiss her again and again. There was no limit to the lusty route his mind took when looking at Sarah, but he had his niece in his arms and he had to remember that as well. He focused his attention on her instead of on Sarah's bountiful cleavage. "Shh, Sarah. Give me a minute. I'll tell you soon as she goes back to sleep."

Sarah's voice softened to nearly a whisper. "She's almost out. I think you can put her down."

Case looked at her and she nodded. "Go on."

Carefully, Case laid the baby on her back and covered her waist-high with a light blanket. Christiana snuggled into her crib, her eyes peacefully closed as she slept.

Case followed Sarah out of the nursery. She stopped and turned briskly. Case bumped into her, a place that was pure heaven and sheer hell as her chest brushed against his. How easy it would be to follow the path his mind had taken, to press Sarah against the wall and finish what they'd started this morning. But her demanding tone put a halt to those appealing thoughts.

"Tell me what that was all about?"

Case stepped back, removing his body from hers. "Fences were knocked down. At least twenty yards, maybe more. I'm sure it was deliberate. I know who did this, Sarah. And I got to thinking of you and the baby up here, all alone, and well…"

Sarah's eyes softened on him. "You were worried?"

"There is a danger, Sarah. I know you don't believe it, but it's true. I had to make sure you two weren't hurt."

Sarah shook her head, an obstinate light coming into her eyes. "I'll thank you for that, but I really don't think anyone is out to harm me…us."

"Sarah." Case laced his voice with warning.

"Okay, okay. But we're fine. I think Uncle Case shocked my daughter right down to her tiny toes, though. She'd never heard you raise your voice before."

Case scratched his head. "I didn't mean to upset her."

"You handled her okay."

Case thought about that a second, realizing he'd done a good job of soothing the little one's feathers. "I did, didn't I?"

"Good thing, too. I've just added to my list of rules. Whoever wakes my child, is obliged to get her back to sleep again. Got that, Jarrett?"

His lips lifted up in a smile but he lowered his voice to a mere whisper. "I'd like to hear the rest of your rules, Sarah."

Sarah blushed, a deep rose coloring her skin that she couldn't disguise. But Sarah never backed down from a challenge. Case loved that about her. "Rule number one. Don't mess with Sarah Jarrett."

"Or what?" he asked, enjoying this a bit too much and he wondered if she meant waking her baby or surprising her with an unexpected kiss. Didn't really matter. He wasn't planning on doing either again.

"Or you'll get more than you bargained for."

Case chuckled. If only she knew that he'd make a deal with the devil for her. If all it took was a bargain to claim Sarah as his, he'd give up a limb or two, but life simply wasn't that easy.

Hell, he couldn't stand here all day gawking at her like a schoolboy with a crush. He had problems on the ranch that couldn't be ignored. He planned to call the sheriff and let him know about the downed fences and his suspicions as to whom might have done it.

"I think I've already gotten much more than I bargained for, Sarah," he said with a wink before heading out the door.

Boisterous cries woke Sarah from a sound sleep. She fought a valiant battle to open her eyes. The penetrating complaints continued on and Sarah sat up. Usually she didn't sleep so soundly, but all those late-night feedings were finally catching up with her, she surmised. "Okay, sweet baby. Mama's coming," she muttered, rising up as quickly as her sleepy form would allow. She donned her cotton robe and didn't bother with slippers. The nights, like the days, had been overly warm lately.

Sarah ambled to the nursery noting that Christiana's cries had become only tiny whimpers. She stopped up short by the door, catching a glimpse of Case, cradling her baby in his arms. With his back to her and from what she could see, he'd enfolded her close against his bare chest—his incredibly fit bare chest. Faded jeans, tossed on in a hurry no doubt, hung low on his hips.

Sarah's mouth went dry.

She'd always known Case was good-looking, a hunk, some women might say, but watching him now, seeing just a hint of his profile in the shadows of the room as he rocked her baby in his arms, did something to her. Something profound, something dangerous and something she would never admit to in the light of day.

This was Case, after all. He was smitten with her little daughter and that was understandable. From Sarah's viewpoint, who wouldn't fall head over heels in love with Christiana? But, Sarah admonished herself for the sensations racing like mad through her body. She called herself a fool, a lonely widow who had been without the love of a good man for quite some time.

That's all it was. Loneliness.

Case turned then, and granted her a smile. Quietly, he said, "Diaper or food?"

Sarah walked into the room, trying hard *not* to stare at his chest or the way his perfectly scattered chest hairs angled down past his navel, dipping into his jeans. "Both, probably."

"I can do one, but the other," he said, glancing at her breasts with a mischievous gleam in his eyes, "is your job."

Sarah tried her best to ignore the stirring his perusal had on her body. But her breasts were sensitive and the slightest sensual suggestion had her nipples pebbling hard. The man usually didn't miss much, but Sarah hoped the dim light and shadows masked her discomfort. She spoke in a hushed tone. "You want to diaper her?"

"I want to *try*."

"You…don't have to."

"I know I don't," he whispered, "but I'm here now and I want to help."

"Sorry she woke you."

"She didn't. I wasn't asleep."

Sarah thought that odd since Case hadn't gone out as he'd planned and they'd both turned in early. Earlier, she'd overheard him calling someone, telling them that he couldn't make it tonight, but he'd see them next week for sure. He'd spoken quietly on the phone, saying something had come up and that it was personal, but he hadn't tried to hide his conversation. He hadn't explained anything about it to her, either. At that moment, she'd known why he hadn't gone out as planned. The downed fences worried him. His sense of duty kept him on the ranch tonight.

She supposed she should be grateful. Instead she felt something far more unsettling pulsing through her veins. And as his male scent, part aftershave, part earthy man, drifted up from his skin to tease her nostrils, Sarah's body heat went up a notch or two. The kiss they shared wasn't far from her mind, and at times like these, in the quiet of the night when darkness beseeched her loneliness, did Sarah wish for things she knew she couldn't have. Case wasn't in her plans for the future. Case was Reid's brother. In her heart and mind, he was strictly off limits. But sometimes, her body forgot.

Sarah drew in a breath and offered him a diaper. "Have at it."

Good-naturedly, Case nodded, setting the baby down on the diaper changer. Sarah stood close by to watch. Occasionally Case's body brushed hers, creating tingles that Sarah tried darn hard to ignore. But to his credit, his full attention was on the job at hand. Once done, he looked to Sarah for approval.

"Pretty good," she said, not mentioning that the diaper was lopsided and the tabs were probably too loose to hold it on for long. She'd fix it later, not to hurt his ego.

Sarah picked up the baby. "I'd better feed her," she said, sitting down on the rocker and waiting for Case to leave.

Case stared into her eyes, then glanced at the baby with a yearning Sarah couldn't answer. She couldn't invite him to stay. She couldn't allow that intimacy. To her way of thinking, having him stay would be far more intimate than the kiss they'd shared and perhaps far more dangerous. She couldn't let her loneliness override her resolve with regards to Case. He wasn't a man she should let into her heart.

Long moments passed before he nodded then finally left the room.

"Goodness," Sarah said softly, "your uncle sure has a way about him."

And Sarah was just coming to realize that she was living with one sexy-as-sin man.

# Six

"I hope we're not interrupting," Bobbi Sue said, standing on the Jarrett doorstep with her young daughter Maureen in tow.

"Heavens, it's good to see you," Sarah said, taking her friend by the arm and sweeping her into the house. She hugged Bobbi Sue then bent to kiss Mo on the cheek. "You two are always welcome." She lifted up to meet Bobbi Sue's gaze. "And what could you possibly be interrupting?"

Bobbi Sue glanced around the front room then her inquisitive gaze darted up the staircase. "Case around?"

Sarah laughed at her friend. Her imagination could rival the most inventive soul on earth. "Case is working, Bobbi Sue. Jeez, you gotta stop watching those afternoon so—" she began, then decided against finishing her thought. Little Mo was listening and she had big ears for such a small child. "Never mind." She waved her thought off and smiled at Mo. "The baby's sleeping. Let's go see her."

Sarah led them to a cozy corner of her big kitchen. Little Mo's eyes grew as wide as silver dollars as she gazed down at the sleeping child. She whispered, "Mommy says to be real quiet around the baby cause she's so little."

"She is, but would you believe she's gained almost two pounds in four weeks? Today is her official due date and she's almost seven pounds."

"She's catching up quick," Bobbi Sue commented, "and isn't she just darling. Oh Mo, I can barely remember when you were that small. Good thing I've got plenty of pictures to prove it. Are you taking lots of pictures of her, Sarah?"

Sarah nodded. "Case is. He's good with a camera."

Bobbi Sue walked away from the bassinet, eyes twinkling. "I bet that's not all he's good at."

"Hush up, Bobbi Sue," she said, glancing back at Mo. Bobbi Sue's daughter hadn't taken her eyes off of the baby. "And stop that."

"Stop what?"

Sarah ran her hands down her face, wondering why she bothered trying to set Bobbi Sue straight. Her friend was determined to make something out of nothing. "Talking about Case like he's my…" Gosh, she couldn't say the words much less think them.

Bobbi Sue shrugged with nonchalance. "He's your brother-in-law."

"Yes, he is," Sarah agreed, hoping Bobbi Sue was finally seeing the light. He was Reid's brother, a man she couldn't get involved with.

"And damn good-looking."

"Bobbi Sue."

"One sexy cowboy," she whispered so Mo wouldn't hear.

Sarah exhaled, shaking her head. She didn't need reminding of that fact. She'd been fighting off lusty thoughts of Case ever since he'd kissed her that day. She hadn't forgotten the impact of his kiss or the protective, heady way he'd held her and made her feel special.

"Just stating the obvious. I'm sure he's got the girls lined up. I mean to say, when he's not doting on you and taking pictures of Christiana."

"Have a seat," Sarah said politely, remembering her manners. Sarah brought a pitcher of iced tea to the table and poured two tall glasses, setting one down in front of Bobbi Sue. Sarah sipped hers then sat down to face her. "First off," she began quietly, noting that Mo was still smitten with the baby, "Case doesn't dote on me. And I can't help it if he likes taking pictures of his niece. Christiana is his flesh and blood, Bobbi Sue. At one time, I had to remind myself of that, but now it's obvious that he's taken with her. He even tries his best to diaper her."

Bobbi Sue let out an animated gasp. "No! Hard-riding rodeo man Case Jarrett wouldn't have the first notion how to diaper a baby. I can't picture it, Sarah. I just can't."

Sarah giggled. "He's terrible at it. I wait until he leaves the room then adjust the diaper so the dang thing won't fall off."

Bobbi Sue shook her head in disbelief. "I wish I could see that."

"And I think you're right about him having the ladies lined up. Well, maybe one for sure. Case wasn't into two-timing a girl, he just had them in succession."

Bobbi Sue set her glass down and leaned in, full of interest. "He's got someone?"

Sarah nodded. Maybe now, her dear imaginative friend would let up on her. "He goes into town every Tuesday night. Never says where he's going."

"Could be a poker game, or a bowling league?"

Laughter erupted that Sarah couldn't contain. She put a hand to her mouth to keep from waking the baby. "Sorry, I just can't see Case in bowling shoes. And he gets with the hands here on the ranch for poker. They meet once a week in the bunkhouse and have themselves a time."

"So, you think he's seeing someone?"

Sarah lifted her shoulders. "It's none of my business."

Bobbi Sue sipped her tea. "He comes home to you, so he's *not* sleeping in town."

Sarah had just about given up on her romance-minded friend. "He comes home to his *ranch*. Don't forget he's half owner. He's got a vested interest here."

"Not waiting up or anything, are you?"

"No, but I'm up at all hours with the baby." She wouldn't add that she'd had to deal with bumping into Case in the nursery many times during the night. Since that first time, the night of the problem with the downed fences, there had been three other occasions where she'd met up with him in the middle of the night. She'd tried her level best to convince him not to bother, explaining gently that Christiana wasn't his responsibility, but that had only brought her a dark angry glare from him. So she'd stopped insisting he not be a part of Christiana's life. As long as he didn't include himself in her life, she'd be fine. No sense, having the man angry with her all the time. Besides, Christiana sure liked her uncle Case.

Bobbi Sue patted her hand. "Then, I'm glad you have Case here. Sounds like he's trying to help out."

"Mommy," Mo interrupted, coming to stand between

Sarah and her mother, "we almost forgot to invite Christiana to my party."

Bobbi Sue's brows lifted. "Oh dear, we can't have that. It's the reason we stopped by. Go on, sweetheart. You do the inviting."

Mo turned to Sarah with big eyes and a hope-filled expression. If she'd asked for the moon, Sarah wouldn't be able to say no to this child. "Can Christiana come to my birthday party on Saturday?"

"Oh, well, sure. The doctor says it's okay to take her out now."

Bobbi Sue chimed in. "Some of Mo's little friends and some of mine are invited for cake and ice cream."

"The baby and I will be there." Sarah smiled to Mo, her best friend's daughter. She couldn't believe it had been five years ago since little Maureen Renee was born.

"And Case, too," Mo added. "He promised to do roping tricks."

"Oh, uh, that's nice." Sarah's excitement deflated, but she wouldn't let Mo see that. More and more, it seemed, Case and Sarah were thrown together. Now, she and Case would be taking Christiana on her first trip off the ranch.

Bobbi Sue added, "Apparently Case promised my little one here, while at your baby shower. She didn't forget it, either. Besides, I'd have included him anyway. He's practically...family."

Reid had been practically family to the Currys, not Case. Had he earned that right by default, because Reid was no longer around? Sarah admonished herself for resenting Bobbi Sue's generous nature. Her friend only had good intentions. "I'll remind him about the roping tricks. I'm sure he'll be able to come, Mo."

Mo grinned from ear to ear and turned when the baby squawked. "The baby's awake."

Sarah took her hand and walked her over to the bassinet. "Looks like she is. And I bet she'd love to meet her new friend."

Sarah picked up the baby and led Mo over to the parlor sofa. "Sit down and I'll put the baby in your lap."

Obediently, with an expression of anticipation, Mo sat down. Carefully, Sarah placed her child in Mo's outstretched arms and the older child cradled her with utmost care.

Bobbi Sue entered the room with Case. "Would you just look at that?"

Case sidled up next to Sarah, putting a hand to her back, the slightest of touches, perhaps only a finger or two, but the impact rattled her clear down to her snakeskin boots. Heat coursed through her veins whenever Case was near and right now hot flutters swamped her from his slightest caress. "Looks like our little Christie has found herself a new best friend," Case said, flashing a quick smile.

*Our little Christie.*

Sarah cringed, hearing those words, knowing she was overreacting. Case had a possessive nature and he hadn't meant it like it sounded. But a quick glance at Bobbie Sue had her wondering.

Her dear friend cast her a smug, see-what-I-mean look that brought fear to Sarah's heart.

Case had railroaded her into this. He knew for a hard cold fact that Sarah didn't want him tagging along into town to buy little Maureen Curry her birthday gift. She'd only asked if he had the time to watch the baby during naptime so she could make a quick trip into town.

Case had used all his powers of persuasion, had given her all the reasons why he thought it best for them all to go. The baby might wake up early and need a feeding. Of course, Sarah had a reserve of milk in bottles for the baby, but Case had convinced her Christie might not take the bottle from him. Then there was the fact that it was a beautiful day, not overly warm with a cloudless blue sky overhead. It would be a damn shame for the baby to miss such an outing. And when Sarah suggested she go out alone, with the baby, Case plastered on his most shocked expression. This was the first trip off the ranch and she'd have a long drive into town. She should start off with an easier trip, one closer to home. And besides all of that, he needed to buy Mo a gift, too, unless Sarah wanted to share a gift with him. She'd thought on that all of one second before shaking her head.

So with a sigh of reluctance, Sarah had relented.

Guilt found its way to his gut, but it couldn't be helped. Case had an uncanny need to spend time with Sarah. He'd been keeping his distance, or trying to, but he'd finally given up, surrendering to his bouts of loneliness. Lonely nights filled with sensual thoughts of the woman sleeping only a few feet away had him hell-bent and edgy. He figured as long as he had to endure the torment, he might as well enjoy her company. And his arguments weren't grounded in lies. He'd really meant all of those things.

Sarah pushed the baby stroller, glancing down the aisle at Kruger's toy store. She picked up a doll and spent time studying it. "I don't know," she said. "I wish I'd have thought to ask Bobbi Sue for a few suggestions. I don't want Mo to be disappointed."

"You think she's into dolls?"

"I sure was at her age, but times are different now."

"I wonder if little Christie will love playing with dolls when she's older."

Sarah smiled. "If she's like her mommy...maybe."

"Maybe I should buy her one now." Case started to peruse all the various dolls on the shelf. Sarah stopped him with a hand to his arm.

"She's too young. These aren't safe for her to play with yet."

"Oh. Right. I guess I'll have to wait until she's five then."

Sarah cast him an odd look, before turning away.

Case spotted a little girl about Mo's age shopping alongside of her mother. He walked over to them. "Would you two mind coming over and checking out the dolls? We're trying to buy a gift for our friend's daughter and—"

"Oh sure," the mother said, seeming to understand their dilemma. "It gets confusing with all the different choices. How old is the girl?"

Case looked at the small child beside her. "How old are you, darlin'?"

"Five."

Case grinned. "Same age. Mind showing us what doll you'd like best?"

The girl smiled and headed over to the doll section. She took only a few moments before pointing to the latest Barbie creation with a full wardrobe included. "That one."

Case lifted the box from the shelf and handed it to Sarah. "What do you think?"

"Perfect," Sarah said, granting the young girl a smile of approval. "Thank you very much."

Her mother took the child's hand and walked over to the stroller by Sarah's side. "Oh, what a sweet baby. Look, Patti, she can't be more than a few weeks."

"She's a month old," Case said quickly, correcting her. The woman glanced up at Sarah.

"She was premature," Sarah explained.

"So petite and so adorable. Won't be long before she'll be telling you both exactly what she wants from Krugers." The woman glanced at Case, then to Sarah. "I've got three. Is she your first?"

"Yes, my first," Sarah responded, and Case could see the explanation on her lips, her readiness to set to right the woman's wrong assumption.

"Well, congratulations to you both. Enjoy your baby. They grow up far too fast. Say goodbye, Patti." And with her farewell, they moved down the aisle.

Case hadn't minded her assumption, but it was evident Sarah had by the frown pulling down her lower lip. "No harm done, Sarah." Was it that distasteful to Sarah that they were thought of as a family? It was an innocent and reasonable mistake made by a stranger.

"No, no harm done," she agreed softly, but Case knew Sarah wasn't telling the truth. The woman couldn't lie worth a damn.

"I'm starving. How about lunch?"

Sarah looked at Christie, gnawing on three fingers. "I'm going to have to feed her soon."

"That's all right. We can pick something up at the café and head over to the park. I'll spread a blanket and we'll have ourselves a picnic. Don't want Christie missing the best part of the day."

That idea pulled Sarah out of her sour mood. "I'm a bit hungry, too. Okay."

A short time later, Case was sorry he'd made the suggestion. He'd endured watching Sarah nurse the baby as discreetly as possible from under a small quilt and as much as he knew he should give her some privacy, Case hadn't been able to tear himself away. He'd fidgeted with arranging the cartons of food on the blanket and opening soda cans, but he'd been watching, fully aware of the scene before him. A serene expression crossed over Sarah's face and as the baby made gurgling sounds, Case's heart tripped over itself. Sarah, holding her baby to her breast, had never been more beautiful to him. Or more unattainable.

Twenty minutes later, with the baby asleep in her infant seat and the food nearly gone, Case stretched out his legs on the blanket. Bracing his face in his hand, he faced Sarah.

"We should go," she said with an anxious edge to her voice, but Case wasn't having any of it. The day was far too gorgeous and selfishly he was enjoying this quiet time with Sarah.

"In a minute or two, darlin'. It's a pretty day and I'm with a pretty lady."

Color rose quickly to Sarah's face. Her cheeks grew pink, contrasting beautifully with the deep blue in her eyes. Case thought he'd stunned her speechless, which would be something, since Sarah always gave as good as she got. Case often wondered what making love to Sarah would be like. Was she as passionate in bed as she was out? Erotic thoughts drifted through his head of running his hands through her silky hair, touching her soft skin, lying naked with her. His body grew tight as a wire. Hell, he had it bad and if he didn't change his way of thinking now, Sarah would witness firsthand, just how bad.

"You think little Mo will like the boots and hat you picked out for her?" he asked.

"I th-think so," Sarah said, her voice wobbly. He

didn't know if it was a good thing or not, that he made her nervous.

"Me, too. You've got good taste. I wouldn't know how to pick out something like that. Thanks for shopping for me."

Sarah smiled, a small all-too-brief lifting of her lips. "You're welcome."

Case remembered those lips, the subtle sexy taste of her, the way she'd given in to him so fully, the way she'd gotten him hot with her tongue and her mouth. God, that mouth. He didn't know how long he'd last on the ranch if he couldn't hold her, if he couldn't kiss her again. There was so much between them, a loved one who had died, a baby delivered, a struggling ranch to run, and although those things should bring them closer together, they seemed to push Sarah further away.

She was afraid of him. Still didn't trust him.

Damn.

"I'm not trying to take Reid's place," he said more harshly than he intended. Hell, he was trying to make a new place with Sarah. Yet, she resisted and he knew how hard it must be for her to open up to him. Didn't help matters that he was Reid's brother. He'd witnessed her guilt at times, during unguarded moments.

Sarah jerked her head up. Bravely she met his eyes. "I know."

"Do you? You sure didn't like it when that lady thought I was your husband today."

Sarah stiffened, belying the casual shrug she tried to produce. "It was only natural to think that, I suppose."

"That might happen often. Living together like we do, on the ranch."

"It's your ranch, too, Case. I can't ask you to leave."

"I wouldn't," he said plainly. Not because he wanted

his birthright so much as he wanted to secure Sarah and the baby's future. The promise he'd made to Reid was never far from his mind.

"Of course. We just have to make the best of the situation."

Now he was a "situation." A surly mood threatened his composure. Anger surfaced, but he tamped it down. Giving Sarah a hard time wasn't his intent.

But the lady sure was giving him a hard time.

Each and every doggone night.

"Yep, we'll make the best of the situation."

Case twirled the rope overhead then swung it out, lassoing the makeshift calf Carl had created with an old wooden sawhorse and a bucket for a head. About a dozen kids, ranging in age from three to ten years old, applauded, asking for more. Case did a few more tricks with the rope, some he'd recalled learning from a talented Navajo he'd met while on the rodeo circuit, others he'd dreamt up on his own. In his spare time, between competitions he'd practiced his roping skills any way he could. But today, he was having a good old time entertaining the kids.

"Now it's your turn," he said. "Who wants to try?"

Case spent the next forty-five minutes working with the older children, teaching them how to make a slipknot and toss the rope, the sawhorse being their target.

"I think you've earned yourself a beer," Carl said, when Bobbi Sue announced that it was time to open presents. "Come on over by the tree and I'll grab us some brews."

Case sat on a bench, legs spread wide, watching Sarah and Bobbi Sue set up the gifts on the porch. Sarah looked beautiful today, wearing a colorful calico summer dress and little red boots. Case figured she was testing out her wardrobe, enjoying the clothes she hadn't fit into for months. But damn, the clothes she wore ''fit'' her shape in a revealing way that had him working up a sweat just from glancing at her. The subtle plunge of her neckline left him imagining a full swell of breasts underneath and the slimness of her waist made him ache to hold her there, to pull her close to his hot body and show her just what she did to him. And those red boots? Hell, he imagined her in them and nothing else.

He watched her laugh with Bobbi Sue, the baby always within her reach, sleeping comfortably. Little Mo and her friends gathered around the pile up of gifts.

Carl handed him a bottle, grinning like the devil.

''What?'' Case scowled at him.

''You ain't taken your eyes off of her since you got here.''

Case sipped his beer. ''Who, Bobbi Sue?'' Case didn't mind rattling Carl's cage. Case could badger like the rest of them.

''Ah, now my wife's a beauty, but you know I'm talking about Sarah.''

Case took a last glance at Sarah then looked away. He gulped down the rest of his beer.

''What are you going to do about it?''

Case shook his head, palming the empty bottle in his hand. ''Nothing.''

Carl pulled back from his place on the bench and laughed heartily. ''Nothing?''

''That's what I said.''

''Okay, gotcha. Nothing. But while you're doing nothing, Sarah might want different.''

Now, Case laughed. It wasn't a joyful sound, but more a snort of disagreement. ''I doubt that.''

"It's true Bobbi Sue's always inventing romance when it don't exist, but I see Sarah clearly. And she's been looking at you different lately." Carl chuckled. "The fact that she's looking at all makes me wonder about her." Carl shoved his shoulder into Case.

Case didn't need to hear this. He didn't need to garner one grain of hope where Sarah was concerned. Damn Carl and Bobbi Sue for their matchmaking ways. Sarah wasn't coming around. She still barely tolerated him. He was on the ranch because he owned half interest, not because Sarah wanted him there. If she could, she'd toss him out, but Case wouldn't leave, no matter how hard Sarah made it for him.

"Trust me, Carl. She ain't looking."

Carl took a minute to study Sarah on the porch. "Might be she's looking, but you're the one who's not doing the *seeing*."

After the party, Case parked the car in front of the house and slanted a look at Sarah, Carl's words echoing in his head. Coming home like this, with Sarah by his side and the baby in her car seat in the back shook Case's resolve.

How easily he'd slipped into "family mode" with them. It hadn't been conscious or deliberate, yet Case had a protective nature when it came to the two females in his life. He wanted Sarah, there was no denying, but it was more than that. And the more he looked at her, the more he realized Sarah was far out of his reach.

"Case?" Sarah said, breaking the silence. She'd noticed him staring, her eyes wary, maybe even puzzled. She didn't know the emotions roiling in his gut, how much she affected him, yet there was sizzling tension in the air. She had to notice the electric pulse radiating between them. Putting her hand on the side door, ready to get out, ready to run, she cast him a tentative smile. "The party was fun, wasn't it?"

"Yeah."

"The children loved your roping tricks."

"Yeah."

She blinked, the soft lashes coming down to caress her cheeks. When little Christie squawked, a tiny complaint to get attention, Sarah tilted her head. "I guess I'd better get the baby in."

"Yeah," he said once again, and swept out of the car, easing Christiana out of her car seat. He handed Sarah the baby and they entered the home they shared, Sarah heading for the baby nursery.

Case stood at the foot of the stairs, raking his hand through his hair, watching Sarah sashay up the steps in her pretty little dress. She turned at the top of the stairs and glanced down at him. "Are you coming up?"

Hell, if that were the invite he'd been wishing for, he'd take the stairs three at a time to be with her. He'd help her put the baby down, then make long, slow, torturous love to her. But Sarah wasn't offering him anything and she never would. "Uh no. Actually," he began, deciding that tonight with his mood, this would be best, "I'm heading over to the Wet Whistle. Some of the boys are throwing Grady Wilkins a shindig. Seems he got himself engaged last week."

"Oh? Anyone we know?"

"I don't know her name. I expect to find out tonight."

Christie wiggled in Sarah's arms, drawing her attention away.

"Sarah?"

She glanced at him.

"You going to be all right, tonight?"

She smiled wide. "We'll be fine, Case. You go on.

We're, uh,'' she started to say, but caught herself. Case didn't want to hear one more time, that Sarah and the baby weren't his responsibility, when every beat in his heart pounded out that they were.

''We're going to have us a nice bath and get to bed early,'' she amended, looking down at the baby. Good thing, too, because Case's imagination had taken flight— Sarah soaking in a tub of bubbles. Hell, he'd better get out of here, fast.

''Good night, Sarah.''

''Good night, Case.''

Nothing like a night out with the boys, Case thought with eager anticipation, to get a man's mind back in proper perspective.

# Seven

---

After a long relaxing soak in the tub, Sarah climbed into bed. She'd put the baby down an hour ago and was eager to close her eyes and get the rest she craved.

But a restless unease completely foreign to her, crept in. An enveloping sensation that had her tossing and turning stayed with her for a good part of the night. Sarah didn't understand it. She willed her body and mind to relax, but it wasn't working. Her practical mind kept screaming, "Go to sleep." She'd learned that in order to keep up with a busy day, she needed to sleep when the baby slept, or pay the consequences.

Yet, Sarah couldn't fight it anymore. She rose from her bed and after checking on her slumbering daughter, ambled downstairs. Perhaps a drink of water or milk might help, she thought. She opened the refrigerator door, but noises, a rattling sound at the back door, startled her to attention. "Who's there?" she called out.

No answer.

The rattling continued.

She remembered that Case wasn't home. He'd gone out drinking with his buddies. Could that be him, trying to get inside the house? Slowly, with cautious steps, Sarah walked over to the door. "Case?"

Again, no answer.

Sarah moved to the window, parting the curtain slightly and her heart nearly stopped. A man in a dark ski mask shot his head around. The whites of his eyes pierced her for one long silent moment then he took off running. Sarah let out a horrific shriek. She stumbled back, clutching her chest as panic engulfed her. She began to tremble, her body reacting to the stark fear rising up.

Someone had tried to break into the house!

It was late, well past midnight. Case wasn't home. Had something happened to him? What if that man, the intruder had hurt Case? Was he lying somewhere on the property, injured, bleeding or worse? Worry set in, mingling with her fears. She recalled all of Case's warnings about the Beckman Corporation trying to buy out their land. Sarah couldn't believe that they'd go to these extremes, to actually attempt a break-in to secure what they wanted. And oh, if it were true, Case could be out there somewhere.

Sarah fought off the fright and ran upstairs to check on Christiana. The baby slept quietly, thank goodness. Sarah grabbed the phone in her bedroom then ran back to the nursery. Blocking the entrance with the diaper changer, Sarah leaned heavily on the wall. The only way to know for sure that Case was all right was to get the sheriff out here.

Pulse racing, she dialed the emergency number and

only when the dispatcher said they'd send someone out to investigate immediately did Sarah take her first calm breath.

Sarah dressed into an old pair of Levi's and plaid shirt then fed the baby one last time. She watched for the lights on the sheriff's car from the upstairs window and once she was certain that he'd arrived with a deputy, she went downstairs to unlock the door. Much later, after the sheriff took his report then assured her that they'd done a complete search for Case and he wasn't on the property nor was his truck, Sarah finally fell into an exhausted sleep.

Case put the key into the lock then turned the knob. Blurry-eyed, he entered the house. Sarah stood in the hallway; her gaze fastened on him, but instantly he knew something was terribly wrong. "Sarah?"

She closed her eyes briefly and when she looked at him again, her body trembled. "Thank God you're all right."

Dumbfounded, Case stared at her. Had she been worried that he'd stayed out all night? "Sarah, I can explain."

Her hand shot up. "No need for any explanations, Case. It's just that I thought something might have happened to you last night."

"Why would you think that?"

Sarah sucked in a breath, struggling to get the words out. Case had a bad feeling about this. A deep sense of foreboding settled in his gut. "Because…because someone tried to break into the house last night."

"What!"

"It's true. The sheriff came out. I thought that you'd

been hurt. You've never stayed out all night before, so I…I, well, I didn't know what to think.''

Guilt and disgust plagued him after hearing what Sarah had gone through last night. She sat down on the parlor sofa and told him everything, her hands trembling, her voice unsteady. He could only imagine how she'd felt when she'd spotted that intruder, knowing she was alone with her baby. Case damned himself to hell and back. ''I should've been here, Sarah.''

''I was scared for Christiana. I'd never felt so helpless before and all I could think about was getting to the nursery. I had to make sure she was safe. I, uh, well all sorts of images popped into my head.''

Case's gut clenched once again, thinking of what Sarah had endured. ''Damn, Sarah. I wish it hadn't happened. I wish I'd been here.''

''Then when you didn't come home? I imagined all sorts of things happening to you.''

Case took Sarah's hand, touched that she'd been worried about him. ''I'm fine, as you can see, but just dog-tired. Didn't get a wink of sleep last night.''

Sarah swallowed then glanced away, her eyes centering on the oak tree outside, the early morning sun making her squint. Case knew immediately what path her mind traveled, but this time she was wrong.

''It's not what you're thinking, Sarah.''

Sarah pulled her hand away from his. With a quick smile, she denied his accusation. ''I'm not thinking anything.''

Hell, he didn't know if he should explain about his love life, or rather lack of, since he'd come home to the Triple R. Sure, women had been calling the ranch, but he hadn't returned their calls or their invitations. He'd meant it when he said he was through running around.

Whether Sarah liked it or not, he had responsibilities on the ranch and he aimed to do it right this time. Besides, no other woman on earth appealed to him. Revealing that fact might put notions in her head about his feelings for her. And they'd all be true. She wasn't ready to hear it. He didn't know if she'd ever be ready.

She had no faith in him. Hell, he couldn't blame her. She'd been frightened half out of her mind last night, and he hadn't been here to protect her. He'd let her down again. Reid, too. "Grady drank himself under the table last night. We couldn't stop him. He wound up sick and needed a nursemaid." Case stuck his finger in his chest. "I got that job, since most of the boys had taken off by then. I had to drive him home."

Sarah's eyes revealed perhaps more than she intended. "You were with Grady all night?"

"Yep, just me and Grady. I made him drink a truck-load of coffee. He's meeting his girl's parents today. He kept saying he had to make a 'good 'pression.'" Case chuckled and Sarah smiled. "Boy, can't imagine him having to bone up to her folks today. He's gonna have himself one humdinger of a hangover."

At least Sarah appeared to believe him. And the relief registering on her face made his heart pound. Had she been a bit jealous, thinking he had female companionship last night? She admitted worrying over his safety.

"I'm sorry, Sarah. I shouldn't have left you. I thought to call, but it got late and I didn't want to chance waking you or little Christie."

"Case, I've told you over and over—"

"Shh," he whispered, stopping her with a finger to her lips. "Don't say it, Sarah. The ranch and everyone on it, *is* my responsibility now. I hope you can forgive me for not being here."

Case smoothed his finger over her bottom lip, before backing away. He'd never felt anything softer, seen anything more enticing and if he didn't leave her now, he'd probably shock the heck out of her by kissing her again.

"Case, there's nothing to forgive. You have your own life. I can't expect you to be here with us all the time."

"Until I figure out what's going on around here, I'm not leaving you alone."

"Really?"

"Yeah, really," he said with reassurance.

A light clicked on in her blue eyes, making them look crystal clear. She didn't seem to mind his pronouncement. She'd been jealous and worried about him, too. But Case couldn't dwell on that right now. He had to get to the bottom of the break-in.

"I'm going to call the sheriff. It had to be one of those Beckman agents, Sarah. They're not going to get away with frightening my family."

And if it were the last thing he'd do, he'd make it up to Sarah for not being here last night.

Foot-stomping music coming from the kitchen sparked Case's attention. He headed that way as the fiddling, down-home tunes of the Dixie Chicks lured him, coaxing a smile from his lips. The smile turned to a full-out grin when he spotted Sarah, cooking up breakfast, swinging her hips and sashaying her way around the room. Case leaned against the door frame, arms folded, legs crossed and watched her dance fluidly to the music.

The woman could move.

And those movements, witnessing her long jean-clad legs bend and twist with rhythm and grace, sent a shock of desire straight to his groin. Case shifted his stance, seeking comfort, willing his body to calm down, yet he couldn't get enough. Couldn't tear his gaze away from Sarah. Catching Sarah in these unguarded moments only made him want her more. Seeing the real woman, the woman free of worry and fear, the woman full of vitality and life, weakened Case's resolve to keep his distance.

It had been two days since the attempted break-in and since that time, Case had spoken at length with the sheriff, put the ranch hands on guard and secured the house with dead-bolt locks. Sarah hadn't wilted like a desert flower. No, she'd bounced back, full of vinegar, her strength and determination always to be admired.

That was the problem. Case admired her. *Was* admiring her this very moment, with jiggling breasts and a glossy sheen of moisture on her body. Case stepped into the room and stood behind her. As yet, she hadn't noticed him. He slipped his hand in hers then twirled her. Laughing eyes met his and she giggled as he turned her around and around.

Too soon, the music stopped. She faced him, rosy-cheeked and nearly out of breath. "Morning, Sarah. What's got you in such a happy mood?"

Sarah brushed a strand of hair off her face, attempting to fit the blond lock back into her long ponytail. Bright-eyed, she greeted him. "Good morning to you. I just had the best sleep of my life. The baby slept through the night for the first time."

Case glanced at little Christie's bassinet. He heard gurgling sounds, but didn't investigate. "No kidding?"

"No kidding. She let her mama sleep, like a good baby."

"I bet you promised her the moon."

"Well, just a real good meal, when she's hungry."

Case peered at Sarah's breasts and arched a brow. He wouldn't mind a happy meal, either, he thought wickedly then wondered what the hell was wrong with him. He'd never witnessed anything quite so beautiful as Sarah nursing her baby, yet his mind conjured up one lusty notion after another. Case swore silently, admonishing himself and changed the subject. "You were always a good dancer, darlin'."

Sarah smiled. "I used to dance quite a bit."

With Reid, neither of them mentioned. "You should do it more often."

"If Christie lets me sleep, maybe I will."

Case walked over to her bassinet. Blue eyes, the color of deep waters stared back at him. The baby dressed up in frilly pink, cooed and the soft sound warmed Case's heart. "Morning to you, too, little beauty." And that protective surge once again, reached up and embraced him. He turned to Sarah. "The ranch hands are all on guard. They'll be looking for any signs of danger. The sheriff said that's about all we can do for now. But I've been thinking about setting up an alarm system."

With a quick shake of her head, Sarah disagreed. "We can't afford one, Case. Those systems are expensive."

Case knew Sarah was right. The ranch was struggling, barely making ends meet. Case had the means to earn a lot of money on the rodeo circuit, but that meant leaving Sarah and Christie alone on the ranch. It just wasn't an option.

"The new locks you installed should help." Then with regret in her eyes, Sarah added, "Darn it, Case. This is Barrel Springs, not the big city. We shouldn't have to cage ourselves in like this. It's what I loved most about living here. There's a sense of community. We have neighbors we can trust. We watch out for each other. I just don't understand."

Case walked over to her. Standing close, he wanted to

take her into his arms and whisper words of reassurance. He wanted to take all the worries off her mind and tell her he'd protect her with his life. "It's the Beckman Corporation, Sarah. They're the intruders. Once we get them out of here, things will go back to normal."

Sarah's shoulders slumped. "I suppose, but you shouldn't have to put your life on hold. I know you're only staying home at night because of the baby and me. That's not fair to you."

She was right. He was staying home because of her, but not out of obligation. There wasn't a woman on this earth he'd rather spend time with, wasn't a place around he'd prefer. "Maybe this is where I want to be."

Sarah searched his eyes for the truth. He could see her indecision, the silent battle she waged to believe him. Trust didn't come easily to Sarah. She'd had years of practice, not trusting him. "Josie called again last night and some woman named Tilly from Denver."

Case ran a hand down his face. "Sarah, Tilly's an old friend. She's married to Drew Barnett. He runs the rodeo out of Denver. And Josie's got to get the message that I'm not interested."

"Aren't you?" she said, moving to get past him.

He took a step to block her way. "No. I told you before, I'm not interested."

Sarah sighed and nodded. When Christie complained, they both knew the conversation was over. "I'd better take her upstairs and feed her. Sorry I didn't get breakfast done, but the coffee is made."

"It's okay," he said. "I'll fix something for myself."

Once she'd picked up Christie and left the room, Case couldn't help but grin. Sarah had been jealous. And she'd worried about him the other night. Rare and unexpected hope surged through him. If Sarah had feelings for him, he definitely wanted to know.

The next afternoon, with Christiana napping, Sarah got out her favorite scented body gel and anticipated a leisurely shower, a chance to pamper her body with a relaxing soak. She undressed quickly and stepped into the shower, the warming flow of water hitting her skin, bringing with it a soothing balm. She took pleasure in coating her body with gel and rinsing clean, only to do it all over again. A sigh escaped, a release of tension, as she relished the sheer luxury of time new mothers often didn't get a chance to enjoy. But Sarah knew she had to be economical with her time. Babies were unpredictable. Just when Sarah thought Christiana would nap, she didn't and when the baby seemed like she was ready to be entertained, she'd nod off. After five weeks they were still learning about each other with every day being an entirely new experience.

Shutting off the water, Sarah towel-dried her hair and listened for the baby. All was quiet. She took a minute to breathe deeply, slowing her pace now that she was certain the baby still slept. She belted a silk wrapper and ambled to the nursery. Immediate panic surfaced when she found the crib empty. "Christiana!"

Sarah raced to her room. No signs of baby. Then she ran into Case's room, stopping up short at the scene before her.

Christiana lay peacefully on the bed in the crook of Case's arms, her slumbering breaths slow and easy. The picture they made together brought sweet tears to her eyes. Both appeared to be napping, big strong Case and tiny little Christie succumbing to an afternoon siesta. A smile surfaced that Sarah couldn't contain. She watched the two of them sleep, wishing for one moment that she could join them on Case's bed. Temptation seeped in and Sarah realized what an inviting vision they made.

Sweet and innocent. Two words she never thought to associate with Case Jarrett, yet there he was handsome as ever, looking as sweet and innocent as her daughter.

Sarah stepped out of the bedroom, leaving them to their nap. She entered her room and headed for the closet to pick out clean clothes. The afternoon shower had been a result of getting off to a late start today, with Christiana fussing all morning. Bobbi Sue mentioned little Mo having had growth spurts, and Sarah figured that was the cause of her daughter's mood earlier. Christiana seemed hungrier, needing more nourishment than ever before.

"Sarah?"

She turned at the sound of Case's voice. Standing just outside her door, he greeted her with a sexy smile. Sleep tousled and hazy-eyed, he entered the room. Sarah found herself backing up, pressing against the closet door, her heart racing. Case didn't appear sweet and innocent anymore. He looked far too appealing and infinitely too dangerous for a lonely woman wearing not much of anything.

"The baby's asleep in my room. I heard your shower running when she was crying, and figured you could use the break. I guess we both dozed off." A crooked smile lifted the corners of his mouth.

"I know," she offered, hugging tight her wrapper. "I walked in on the two of you napping."

Case took a leisurely tour of Sarah's body, piercing her with a look that curled her toes. "You should have joined us."

The minute he said the words, Case's mind flashed an image of Sarah lying next to him on his bed. He was fully awake now, in instant alert mode and completely taken by the woman haunting his dreams. Pure male instinct told him that Sarah wore nothing underneath that silky wrapper. Moisture pooled at the tips of her breasts, jutting the material out, outlining the fullness, the pebble hard peaks. His body grew hard immediately and his mind worked overtime imagining pulling at the ties of that silk robe she wore.

"I...wasn't dressed."

"I can see that," he offered honestly, and what he did see through that light robe made him ache for her all the more.

"Oh." She drew in her lower lip.

"You look pretty in blue, Sarah. Brings out all the sparkle in your eyes." He took a step closer, his eyes locked with hers. When he reached her, he extended his arm to lift a strand of her hair and study the golden lights he found there. "You were wearing blue the night of the prom." He probed her for an answer. "Do you remember?"

Sarah nodded, her beautiful blue eyes lifting to his.

"I never forgot, either, darlin'."

"Case, it'd be better if we didn't talk about it."

"I agree," he whispered, his hand caressing the softness of her cheek, "no more talking." He bent his head, looked deep into her eyes then claimed her mouth with crushing passion. And a profound buried hunger emerged instantly within him.

He grasped her waist and yanked her up against the solid strength of him. Sarah let out a little pleasured sound and wrapped her arms around his neck. He ran his hands through her hair, his fingers weaving, tugging, urging, as he blistered her with endless kisses.

"God Sarah, I could never forget you," he uttered urgently, then drove his tongue into her mouth. Sweet sensations poured in, blasting him with heat and desire and wiping clean any memory Case might have had of other women. Sarah was the only woman for him.

And Case knew Sarah had feelings for him, too. She just wouldn't admit them, but the way her body trembled told him all he needed to know. She would have stumbled if he hadn't had such a powerful hold on her.

He kissed her boldly, intimately, tempering his passion with gentle thunder. And when kissing her wasn't enough, Case moved his kisses down her throat, moistening, caressing and licking, his mouth traveling on a sensual journey. The anticipation of what was to come had Case's mind reeling. With expert finesse, Case parted the soft silk of her wrapper, exposing the deep valley of her breasts. She arched toward him, a willing victim to his assault.

Loud boisterous cries from the other room, echoed against the walls. Sarah stilled instantly. Case, too, stopped and lifted his head to listen.

"It's the baby," she whispered needlessly.

Case let out a deep breath.

"I'd better go to her."

Case nodded and took a step back. As she moved to pass him, he tugged on her belt, freeing the material. The wrapper parted down the middle, tempting him, but Case only looked deep into her eyes. "This isn't finished," he said.

Sarah shot him a glance, her eyes filled with regret. "It has to be," she said, and at the moment Case knew by the look of reproach on her sweet face that she'd meant it.

Case cursed his bad luck once again, falling for his brother's girl.

# Eight

Sarah couldn't believe her eyes. Within the span of twenty-four hours, she'd spoken with her sister on the phone, picked her up from the airport and now sat facing her with the late afternoon sun streaming through the kitchen window. "I can't believe you're really here."

Delaney smiled, holding her new niece in her arms, her eyes glowing with warmth. "I couldn't wait to see the baby, Sarah. I had to come. This little girl," she said, gazing down at Christiana, "is just about the sweetest baby in the entire world."

Sarah smiled, too, and her heart filled with joy. She'd been so confused lately, struggling to keep a handle on her place here at the Triple R. Just when she'd thought she had it all figured out, Case Jarrett would do something to shake up her world.

Yesterday's kiss, for one, had been so darn unexpected. Maybe if she'd had fair warning, she'd have stopped it from ever happening. Yet, last night while trying to sleep her mind conjured up images of Case, the warmth of his lips, the heat of his body, the fiery passion that had been simmering beneath. Sarah had felt all those things, too. She'd secretly wanted more from him. He'd made her feel things she hadn't felt in such a long time.

But Sarah knew her reaction to him came from loneliness. She hadn't been held by a man, for a long time. She hadn't been kissed so expertly, either. That's all that it was, a longing that she'd been denied since the death of her husband. And now that Delaney was here, she could put all that behind her. Her sister would be the distraction she needed. For a few days, at least, she wouldn't have to deal with Case Jarrett and the power of his kisses.

"I'm so glad you came *now*." Unintentional desperation lingered in Sarah's voice. She hoped Delaney hadn't picked up on it. She really needed her sister here, to keep her sane, to keep her from thinking about Case and how his presence in the house had been affecting her lately. Getting involved with him would be a disaster. There was just too much at stake. Delaney held the best reason of all, tenderly in her arms at the moment.

*"Now?"*

"Yes, well, you know, because of Gram's birthday and all." That was partly the truth. It was the anniversary of her grandmother's birthday. And the beloved, slightly eccentric woman made them promise not to grieve for her on her birthday, but rather to go out on the town. Of course, going out on the town for Sarah and Delaney usually meant dinner and a movie, but somehow, the two of them felt they were carrying out their grandmother's wishes.

"Oh, yeah. It did work out perfectly, didn't it?"

"And you brought the brooch?" Sarah asked, knowing Delaney wouldn't forget such an important component to their yearly ritual.

"Of course. Jeez, I haven't worn it since we did this last year."

"I haven't worn my ring, either. I used to wear it on my wedding anniversaries."

Delaney reached for her hand. "And you wore it on the day you were married. I'm sorry, honey."

"Only happy occasions, Gram used to say. So, no being sorry, okay?"

Delaney smiled, a quick flash that reminded Sarah of their younger days, when they'd get themselves in a pickle and Delaney would find a way out. "Sure."

"I'll wear it tomorrow when we visit Gram's grave and have our day together. That's what Gram wanted, for us to be together."

"Happy times, only." Delaney winked. "We'll have us a real good time tomorrow."

"Yeah, Gram would like that."

Florie Barnes Johnston, their grandmother, had led quite a life. The daughter of a wealthy oilman, she'd run away from home to marry Sarah's grandfather. There'd been bad blood between the families and Florie had been cut off from the family funds. But she'd been happy with Henry Johnston, blissfully happy and never regretted her decision to become his wife. She'd come away from all that wealth with only two things of value. Delaney owned one, a diamond and emerald brooch, dating back over one hundred years. And Sarah owned the mate, a ring made of similar square-cut emeralds and diamonds. Both were exquisite and both were treasured, the inheritance being more about the love they'd had for the woman who'd helped to raise them, than about the actual monetary value.

The baby's cries brought Sarah back to the present. Delaney handed her over. "She wants her mommy. Feeding time."

"Yes, she's a growing girl."

Sarah unbuttoned her shirt and gently placed the baby to her breast. Suckling sounds resounded in the room and Delaney laughed. "She's a hearty one."

Sarah glanced at the blue-eyed treasure in her arms. "I'm so grateful for that."

Delaney shook her head. "I still can't believe that Case delivered her in your car. You must have been so scared."

Sarah became thoughtful. "I was, at first. But Case was wonderful about it. He kept assuring me that it was going to be all right. He held my hand when I needed him, and after a while, I just placed all my trust in him. We delivered her together."

"We *are* talking about Case Jarrett, the man you can't stand. The man who, who—"

"I never said I can't stand him," Sarah said, her voice elevating. "Where did you get such a notion?"

Delaney's eyes bugged out. "Are you forgetting what he put you through when you were kids? And what about what he did to you the night of your prom?"

"We were so young then, Del."

"Are you defending him?" An incredulous tone came into her sister's voice.

Sarah sat back and glanced down at her daughter. "I'm grateful to him. He's been good to Christiana and me. That's all I'm saying."

A gleam brightened Delaney's eyes. "You're living with him now. This might prove interesting."

"Wrong. We're living in the same house. There *is* a difference." At least that's what Sarah kept telling herself. Yet, often her mind would drift off, and she'd daydream about Case, about being in his arms, about the thrilling sensations he evoked from her with just a look or that darn killer smile or a wildly wicked kiss.

Delaney sat contemplating, which in Sarah's estimation could be a dangerous thing. "Hmm. I think there's more to it than that," Delaney stated point-blank.

Sarah admonished her sister quickly. "Oh, no. Don't you even let that thought cross your mind."

The problem was, those thoughts had not only crossed Sarah's mind, but they were beginning to take up permanent residence there.

"He may not be my idea of the perfect man, Sarah, but he's sexy as hell."

A flash of heat burned Sarah's cheeks. She couldn't deny her sister's allegation. More so now than ever before, Sarah had begun to realize just how appealing Case Jarrett was...in the flesh. Sarah flinched inwardly and shook that thought off.

Her sister wiggled her eyebrows. "You're not saying anything."

"Nope."

"Which means you're not disagreeing."

Sarah drew a breath then let the air out slowly. Delaney knew her too well so arguing the point would get her nowhere. "Case hasn't changed in that regard. He's always held...appeal."

"Hmm." A disapproving frown pulled her lips down as she studied Sarah.

"Stop looking at me that way."

"If he hurts you, that man won't have to worry about breaking bones while busting broncos. I'll do it for him."

Sarah giggled at the absurdity. Her five foot three petite older sis wouldn't know the first thing about breaking bones, but Sarah had to admire her gumption. She was just trying to protect her. "He won't hurt me, Del. There's nothing between us."

But the conversation immediately ended when Case entered the room. "Afternoon ladies." He walked over to the refrigerator and grabbed a pitcher of iced tea. He busied himself with pouring a tall glass.

Delaney bent her head and came as close to Sarah as possible. She whispered, an almost inaudible mouthing of words, "Does he always dress that way?"

Sarah closed her eyes, shaking her head. Gracious, Delaney was supposed to distract her from Case, not make her even more aware of him. It was obvious Case had just showered; his dark hair had been slicked back and the scent of fresh lime soap entered the room when he'd walked in. Barefoot, wearing faded blue jeans that hugged his form to perfection, an equally tight ribbed sleeveless white T-shirt and sporting a day-old beard, Case was a man a woman couldn't quite ignore. Bulging bronzed muscles wouldn't allow it.

*Sexy as hell.*

"Howdy, Case," Delaney said in a mock western drawl. "Will you be joining us for dinner or do you have a hot date tonight?"

With her back to Case, Sarah shot her sister a stern look.

Case's chuckle sounded more like a snort. "No hot dates for me anymore. I gave those up on the rodeo circuit. We've got a mare ready to foal, so I guess I'm in tonight. I want to make sure Pretty Girl has an easy time of it."

Sarah removed the baby from her breast and buttoned

up. When Case walked over, she mustered her courage and looked into his eyes. She'd been avoiding him ever since they shared that powerful kiss, but she knew she couldn't evade him forever. Having Delaney here as a buffer really helped. "You think it'll happen tonight?"

"Could be. It's her first, so I want to be here if it happens tonight."

Delaney offered with a smile, "Seems you're pretty darn good at birthing, Case. From what Sarah tells me."

Sarah and Case looked at each other, their eyes locking with certain understanding and his voice, a soft caress to her ears. "We did all right, didn't we, Sarah?"

Sarah nodded, glancing down at the baby. "Sure did."

Case came closer and bent down. He placed his index finger on Christiana's cheek. "Hello, little beauty." The baby responded to his voice, her eyes focusing on her uncle.

"She needs to be burped," Sarah declared, trying to ignore Case's close proximity, the scent of lime on his skin, the way his dark eyes lit up looking at her baby.

"I'll do it," Case said, reaching for her.

Sarah stifled a giggle when Delaney's mouth dropped open. But then Case's hand brushed Sarah's breast as he took the baby from her arms and her amusement changed to instant sizzle. Her sensitive nipples peaked from the slight touch and heat ran rampant through her body. Case cast her a quick apologetic smile before lifting Christiana up.

"Here, you'll need this." Sarah handed him a pink and yellow receiving blanket to protect his clothing. With care, he placed the baby over his shoulder, rocked her back and forth and patted her back.

The contrast of strong virile man and little helpless baby struck a deep chord within Sarah. Case held Christiana as if she was a fragile flower, protectively, posses-sively, and the baby loved it.

Watching them together put an ache in Sarah's heart. She had never in her life witnessed a more heart-warming scene. Nibbling on her lip, she turned away to stare straight into the knowing eyes of her sister.

"He loves that baby," Delaney said, after Case burped the baby quite successfully then left to check on the mare. "And he can't seem to take his eyes off one certain fe-male."

"I know. Christiana feels the same way. She's already formed an attachment to her uncle."

"I was talking about you, little sis. Case wants you. And it appears our sweet little Christiana isn't the only female on this ranch who's fond of him. So what are you going to do about it?"

Sarah busied herself with changing the baby's diaper, refusing to answer her sister's ridiculous question. She wasn't going to do anything about anything where Case Jarrett was concerned.

*This isn't finished.*

His words echoed in her ears. She'd been taken by surprise by Case when he'd kissed her, both times, but she'd be on guard now and much more prepared. She wouldn't allow her bouts of loneliness to sway her again.

*It has to be.*

And Sarah had meant every word.

Case was beat. He'd spent most of the night in the barn, looking after the mare and when it appeared she'd wait another day to deliver, he'd finally gotten a few hours of sleep. Tossing on a pair of jeans and a T-shirt then splashing water on his face, he went downstairs, being drawn by female laughter. But once he'd heard where the conversation was heading, he stood just outside the door, waiting.

"No way, Delaney. I'm not going to buy *that* kind of lingerie."

"*You* aren't. I'll buy it for you. Think of it as a gift for giving me the sweetest little niece. We're going to stop in on that new shop I saw in town yesterday, Cuddle Up. Gram would have loved that store. The name alone, says it all. You know Gram would approve."

"But *I* don't. I've never worn that sort of thing."

"All the more reason, honey. You've got a gorgeous figure. If I didn't love you so much, I'd hate you. It took me a whole year to get my shape back, and you did it in weeks. So, you might as well celebrate with a silk teddy or a satin negligee. C'mon. Let your sis treat you to something sinfully sexy."

Images of soft satin caressing Sarah's body flashed through Case's mind. A vision of some skimpy female garment meant to torture a man poleaxed his brain. Sweat broke out on his forehead and a noisy groan escaped his throat.

"What's that?" Delaney asked.

Caught, Case walked into the room, the picture of composure. "Just me. My finger got stuck in the door-jamb," he fibbed, waving his hand from the imaginary pain.

Then he glanced at Sarah. She was dressed in all white from her western hat down to her snowy leather boots. A soft lacy blouse, cut full with frill at the neckline and wrists, tapered into a long flowing skirt brought visions to mind of an angelic cowgirl. Case had never seen Sarah look more beautiful. He hadn't seen her in her going-out clothes since he'd moved home. And now that he had the sexy images from before were replaced by quick flashes of flowery bouquets, shining altars and three-tiered cakes, all pristine and puffy-cloud white.

He shook that thought off, blinking his eyes.

"Case, you look pale," Delaney said with concern. "You must have really hurt that finger."

"Uh, no. I'm fine. You both look gorgeous."

"Thank you," Delaney said. Sarah smiled and the baby cooed.

"We're off to visit Gram, then for a day of play."

"Where are you ladies heading?"

Delaney's eyes brightened. "Well, there's this new shop in town that I'm dying—"

"Uh," Sarah interrupted, "we'll be home for supper. We'll have a little lunch and then do some shopping."

A glint of green caught his eye and he walked over to Sarah, lifting her hand to gaze at her ring. It was the only thing she wore that wasn't white. "Your gram's ring?"

"Yes. I only wear it on certain occasions. Delaney's got the mate." Case glanced at Delaney, noticing the diamond and emerald brooch adorning her dress. "Gram wanted it that way."

Case shot Sarah a sincere smile and released her hand. "I'm sure your gram's looking down on you both now with a big smile."

"Yep. She's wishing she could come do the town with us, right Sarah?"

"That's Gram. Only she'd probably find something more exciting for us to do than lunch and a shopping spree. She had bundles of energy."

"She was quite a lady," Case said, remembering Sarah's grandmother. Feisty and overly protective, she'd nearly skinned Case's hide when she'd figured out what had happened between him and Sarah the night of the prom. She'd waited for him outside the ranch one day, and read him a wagonload of grief. Case couldn't blame her, but just like with Sarah, he couldn't tell her the truth, either. But, somehow, Case always suspected, she knew. She'd been a wise old owl.

"Yes," Sarah agreed, "quite a lady."

"Well, have yourselves a real nice day. I've got to check on Pretty Girl. Maybe by the time you return we'll have a new filly or colt."

Sarah frowned, a look of concern on her face. "Maybe I should stay home and help with her. You don't have time to baby-sit the mare."

"I'll do fine, Sarah. You go on. Have a nice day with your sis."

Delaney took Sarah's arm. "Come on, honey. Get the baby and let's go, before the boss man changes his mind."

Sarah shot Case one last guilty look. "Are you sure?"

"I'm sure. I'll come get you later, if she decides to foal."

"Promise?"

"I promise."

Well, at least that was one promise Case could keep. His willpower at an all-time low, Case struggled with his emotions regarding Sarah. One minute he's thinking of making soul-searing love to her in sexy lingerie, the other, he's imagining a small chapel, a long flowered aisle way and pure and innocent wedding white.

Both scared him and both left him wanting.

And neither was *ever* going to happen.

The next day went from bad to worse. Sarah lowered her weary body down on the front steps of the house and leaned against the post, needing the support for her body, her spirit all but broken.

She'd said a tearful goodbye to Delaney this afternoon before Case had driven her to the airport. And while they were gone, Sarah had a visit from Mr. Leroy Coolidge, the banker who held the note on the loan to their ranch.

The ranch debts had been mounting and they'd had to default on the mortgage payments for a few months, but they'd always made due. They'd always found a way. Mr. Coolidge didn't seem to see it that way. He couldn't grant them any more time. Plainly he wanted his money. He knew about the generous offer they'd received from the Beckman Corporation and urged Sarah to sell. The bank couldn't carry the loan without a substantial payment in the next few weeks. "You need to catch up on all the payments from the last months before we can talk again," he'd said, patting Sarah's hand. "You call me in a few days and let me know what you decide."

What decision could Sarah possibly come to? She just plain didn't have the money.

She'd had so many hospital bills to pay for Reid and even with the money Case had sent from his winnings on the rodeo circuit and the little their insurance plan had paid out, it hadn't been near enough. Sarah had had no choice but to take out a second mortgage on the ranch. Now, their debt to the hospital was paid, but that left both the first and second mortgage to deal with.

Leaning her head back, Sarah closed her eyes and tried to gain some sense of peace. It had been a tumultuous year, with losing Reid so unexpectedly, having his child, and now facing financial ruin on the ranch he'd loved so much.

When Sarah opened her eyes, Case was standing right in front of her, wearing a worried expression. She hadn't even heard him drive up. "Sarah, what's wrong?"

"Oh…did everything go okay with Delaney? Did her flight leave on time?"

"Yeah, Delaney's just fine. She said she'll call you tonight."

"Thank you for taking her."

"Sarah?" Case took a seat at the other end of the steps and leaned his back against the post. "Something's wrong."

She nodded and looked out at the Triple R, seeing it the way she'd always seen it…as her future, her baby's future. The land, so vast and untried, nurtured the animals, the livestock that was their livelihood. And the people, Pete and the others who'd been loyal even when they'd had to shave down their pay or offer part-time work to some, had still stayed on. Sarah let out a deep sigh filled with anguish. She was meant to live here. She loved Red Ridge Ranch with all of her heart. She'd wanted her daughter to live here as well. But that didn't seem possible now. Her heart breaking, she turned to Case. "We have to sell the ranch."

Case snorted outright, giving no credence to Sarah's comment. "No way, darlin'."

Sarah spent the next ten minutes explaining to Case everything Mr. Coolidge had stated. His financial demands had to be met in the next few weeks or they'd have to foreclose.

Case took the news with belligerence. "No way," he said, again. "I'm going over the books again tonight. Don't worry, Sarah. We'll find a way out of this mess."

Case left then heading for the barn. Sarah watched him leave, his long strides heading with purpose to check on Pretty Girl. Sarah couldn't even get excited at the prospect of the mare going into labor. If the worst happened, the mare, her foal and all that they owned would soon be in the hands of the Beckman Corporation.

Case had never seen Sarah so distraught. Earlier today, her face had held no hope, her usual bright eyes, held no light. He stood outside her bedroom door very late that night, debating on whether to wake her or not. He knew she needed her sleep, being a new mother and all, but he'd promised. And damn it all, at least he'd keep this promise. He knocked, hoping the news would bring Sarah out of her slump. "Sarah, darlin', the mare had her a brand-new colt."

"Case, just a minute," she said and a moment later, opened her door. She stood there, wrapped in a robe, looking pale and defeated. Case wondered if she'd slept at all tonight. "Pretty Girl had a colt?"

"Yeah, come see him. He's a beauty."

Sarah hesitated, nibbling on her lip like she always did when she couldn't decide something. "C'mon," he said, reaching for her hand. "You've got to see him."

Sarah smiled then, a small lifting of her lips. "Okay," she agreed.

Case kept her hand in his as they descended the stairs and went out the back door to the barn. He drew her up close when they spotted the colt, full of gusto on spindly lean legs that barely held him upright. "See what I mean? He was born less than an hour ago and he's up and prancing around already."

Sarah leaned her head on his chest, but her focus, her full attention was on the colt. In her weary state, Case doubted she even knew that she was leaning on him. But he'd relish the feel of her soft hair brushing his throat, her slow breaths against his chest. Holding her, watching the colt take his first awkward steps in the dead of the night was the most intimate thing Case had ever done with Sarah. He didn't want this time to end. "Oh, Case. He's so perfect. We'll have to think of a good name for him."

Case agreed. "I'll leave the naming up to you."

"I like the white marking against his chestnut snout. And all of his socks are white, too. He's so…striking."

"Hmm, he is."

"*Striker*. That's what we'll name him."

Case grinned. "I like that, Sarah."

Sadness stole over Sarah's face then and Case felt her body sag. "I hope we don't lose him. I hope we—"

"Shh, Sarah."

"Did you find anything we overlooked in the books?"

Case squeezed her hand and pressed her body closer. "No. But I'm not giving up hope, darlin' and neither should you. I'll find a way out of this mess." Case had an ace up his sleeve, but he couldn't get Sarah's hopes up yet. Not until he was sure he could pull it off.

But when Case turned to her, silent tears streamed down her face. "Hey," he said softly, "don't cry, sweetheart." Her tears tore his heart in two. Sarah was a fighter, and to see her like this, so…defeated, just didn't sit well.

He lifted her chin with a finger to gaze into swollen teary eyes. "It's going to work out." He bent his head and kissed her lips softly, a kiss meant to reassure. Sarah sighed raggedly and kissed him back, falling into his arms, crushing her body closer. He enfolded her into his arms and claimed her mouth, delving deeper, surprised by the intense passion with which Sarah responded. He stroked her tongue, and she whimpered, bringing heat and powerful desire with that sound.

Case groaned. He could only take so much. He'd been

dreaming of Sarah, of holding her tight and kissing her again. He'd been dreaming of lying naked with her, making heart-stopping love to her.

Their lips met again and again, Sarah's body pliant against him, her need evident as she worked her fingers through his hair, kissed him frantically and told him in every way, what she wanted from him. He ran his hands all over her body, touching her in ways that made his pulse race out of control. She moaned and whimpered and encouraged him with her mouth and the sweet rub of her body. Case was dying. Every damn fantasy he'd ever had about Sarah was beginning to come true.

But his mind recoiled. This was *Sarah*. He couldn't take advantage of her vulnerable state. She was distraught and scared, that much, he understood. He couldn't throw caution to the wind and give to her, what he'd dreamed about for years. "Whoa, darlin', slow down. I'm only human. Maybe we should stop before this goes too far." His breaths came out ragged and labored. It would be days before he got over this. Days, before he'd stop calling himself every kind of fool for putting an end to this.

Sarah's heart pounded rapidly as she looked into Case's dark solemn eyes. There was a powerful need inside her, a need to escape, a need to be set free, a need to forget all her troubles. She'd been overwrought with emotion for one entire year, her heart being torn to shreds. Yet, she'd been the responsible one, dealing with deaths and debts and ranch problems. She'd held up the best she could, but now, it was as though it was all crashing down upon her.

She *needed*. So badly.

"I'm only human, too, Case." She lifted her eyes to his, her heart, exposed.

"I know, sweetheart," he said, holding her, gently

stroking her hair. His touch brought tremors of excitement, his body brought thrills and her mind simply shut
down. Sarah was tired of being responsible. She was so
doggone tired of always being on guard. Tonight, she
needed to forget. She needed to feel like a woman again.
She needed…Case.

"Ah, Sarah, there's nothing I wouldn't do for you."

Bravely, boldly and without regret, Sarah stepped back
a bit, undid the tie of her robe and let the material drop
to the ground, exposing the black lace teddy Delaney had
insisted on buying her. Sarah sighed deeply, her voice a
shaky plea. "Then don't stop, Case."

"Sarah," he said, taking her hand. His hot gaze raked
her over from head to toe, bringing heat and passion with
eyes dark with intense appreciation. He swore, low, under
his breath. "Damn. You're so beautiful."

Sarah swiftly took in a breath. She needed to hear that,
to know that she was still a desirable woman. She stood
before him, waiting, noting indecision in his eyes for one
brief second, a small battle raging. Then he drew her
close, kissed her soundly on the lips and led her over to
the far end of the barn. He laid out a blanket and brought
her down upon it with him, his eyes searching hers.
"Sarah, I won't deny either of us this, but if you want
to change your mind…"

She shook her head. "I'm not going to change my
mind." She brought her arms up to wrap around his neck,
drew him close and kissed him on the lips explaining
without benefit of words, what she desperately needed
from him. Tonight, she didn't want to talk or think. She
only wanted to *feel*.

Case had the power to do that, to make her feel vital
and alive again. She broke off the kiss and began undoing
the buttons on his shirt. Once done, she spread his shirt

out and over his shoulders. He helped by shrugging it off and tossing it aside. Sarah touched him then, moving her palms over his hot skin, bending her head to kiss his chest, the spiral hairs tickling her cheek.

"Sarah." Case groaned with pleasure, an animal sound of dire want that had him pressing her down on her back and removing the nearly sheer teddy in just seconds. In the back of her mind, Sarah thought the man experienced in removing women's clothes, but she didn't dwell on that, only on the erotic sensations Case's hands grazing her skin evoked and the thrill his lips elicited traveling over her body. Heavens, Case Jarrett knew what he was doing.

The rub of his palms over her breasts brought shocks of heat, the teasing way he fingered her peaks, brought sharp acute tingles. Finally he brought his mouth down to moisten the tips.

Case kissed her over and over, licking at her lips, stroking her center with smooth, urgent caresses, readying her for his entry, until Sarah was ready to burst.

When he tossed off his boots, shrugged out of his pants, and rose above her, Sarah witnessed his strength once again in the firmness of his chest, the power of his arms and the sheer sensual beauty on his face. This is what she needed. *He* was what she needed. There was no turning back. No regrets or guilt. She'd banished all those feelings for tonight. Eagerly she rose to meet him. He pressed inside her slowly, letting her adjust to him, to the newness of it all. "I don't want to hurt you, sweetheart."

Sarah slammed her eyes shut. No, he wouldn't hurt her physically. He'd made sure of that with expert caresses and patient loving. But he had the power to hurt her emotionally, only Sarah didn't want to think about that right now. Tonight was all about forgetting. She opened her eyes to meet his gaze and spoke calmly. "You won't, Case. I know you won't."

He moved inside her with caution and Sarah let him know with a smile or a pleasured sound, she was all right. Case rode her body with finesse, giving as much pleasure as he took. Sarah's heart raced, her body trembled and when Case brought her to the limit, dragging out the inevitable to see to her needs first, she called out into the night, a piercing cry of relief and pleasure and satisfaction.

Case held her, kissed her gently, and wrapped her in his arms as they lay together quietly, each one, she presumed, deep in thought over what just happened. She wanted to stay that way all night, enfolded in his protection, in his vast strength, but she couldn't and she knew that the light of day would bring repercussions. "I have to go," she said softly. She sat up and began gathering her clothes.

"*Don't,* Sarah." Case lifted up, watching her. And she had the distinct feeling Case didn't just mean for her not to leave him at the moment. He'd meant for her not to retreat, not to find fault in what they'd just done. Sarah's heart and mind clouded with mixed emotions. She'd made love with Reid's brother, a man she still didn't know if she could trust. She'd needed him tonight, but she wasn't sure if she'd made a mistake in coming to him. Were loneliness and despair all that brought her to this point?

"I have to, Case. The baby might wake up."

Sarah threw on her robe and dashed toward the door.

"You gonna be all right?" Case stood and called to her.

Sarah cast the handsome cowboy one last glance then left him without an answer. Because the truth was, she honestly didn't know.

# Nine

Sarah,
*I'm leaving early this morning, didn't want to wake you. I'll be gone for a while, taking care of business. Pete is staying at the bunkhouse so you won't be alone. Kiss Christie for me and take care until I see you again.*

*Case*

Sarah stared at the scribbled note Case had left under a magnet on the refrigerator. She'd reread the darn thing for the past three days. Waiting, holding out hope.

But she hadn't heard from Case other than a brief message on her answering machine on the first day. He hadn't said much then, either, except to leave a number where he could be reached if she needed him. He'd gone to Denver.

Sarah ran a hand down her face, trying to put her faith in Case, but failing miserably. He'd left the ranch, didn't say why he'd left or when he'd be back, or *if* he'd be back.

Heavens, she'd practically thrown herself at him the other night, asking him to make love to her. She'd needed him that night, hadn't really given him an option. But now, she was sorry she'd succumbed to those desolate feelings, because Case had run out on her. She felt every bit a fool for giving in to her loneliness and to the sharp pangs of desperation at the prospect of losing the ranch. That night, she'd needed to be held, to be protected, to be loved. But now she knew she'd acted rashly, completely without regard to the consequences.

But she'd never expected this. She'd never expected Case to leave, without much explanation. Had she scared him off? Had it all been too much for him? Each day that passed without hearing from him made it clear in her mind that he couldn't be trusted. He wasn't a man she could rely on. He wasn't a man who stayed. For that one night, she'd forgotten.

When the telephone rang, she jumped. Pushing her body away from the kitchen counter, Sarah answered the phone. "Hello."

"Good morning, Mrs. Jarrett. Leroy Coolidge here. I haven't heard from you and it's been three days. I do need an answer. Are you willing to take my advice and sell the ranch or have you come up with another way to pay down your loan?"

"Uh, hello Mr. Coolidge. Well, I..." Sarah stumbled, searching for the right words, and then inspiration hit. It wasn't something that hadn't crossed her mind before, but now Sarah knew that she was out of options. She hadn't heard from Case again and there just wasn't any other way to pay off the debts. "Actually, I will have a large sum of money to apply toward the loan. I'm asking you to give me until tomorrow morning. I'll come by your office with a check.''

"Make that a money order. And tomorrow will be just fine.''

"Right, a money order. I'll see you tomorrow then. Goodbye.''

Sarah hung up the phone slowly, blinking back tears. She had to do this. For Christiana's sake. She couldn't dwell on what would be lost, only what would be gained. And she couldn't rely on Case, wherever he was. He'd let her down once too many times in the past. For all she knew he'd gone back to the rodeo circuit, missing the excitement of the ride, the thrill of hearing an adoring audience cheer him on.

He'd been good with the baby; she'd give him that, trying his best to fit in as "uncle'' material. And little Christiana had taken to her uncle like a kitten to creamed milk. Sarah had begun to believe that he truly wanted to become a part of the ranch again. That maybe he cared. That maybe, she and the baby had a little something to do with that.

But in her heart, Sarah knew Case wasn't a man who stuck around when the going got tough. She'd been too caught up in his smoldering dark eyes and her own loneliness to remember that. But, she vowed never to forget it again.

She picked up the phone and punched in Bobbi Sue's number, certain now, this was the only way. "Hi Bobbi Sue. I need a big favor. Could you come over here for a few hours to watch the baby? There's something important I have to do.''

"What do you mean you sold your grandmother's ring?'' Case's stormy expression matched the cold steel in his eyes. Just minutes ago, he'd strolled into the house pretty as you please holding a big manila envelope in his hand, wearing a smile, ready to give her a kiss. But Sarah flinched from his advances and explained to him about Mr. Coolidge's demands. "Damn it, Sarah! Why the hell did you do that?"

Sarah had never seen Case so angry. She was still getting over her surprise at his return. Fury spread his nostrils wide and the scar on his face seemed to stretch to its human limits. "I told you why and please keep your voice down. I just got Christiana to sleep."

"And I told you, I'd take care of it!" Case paced the floor, raking his hands through his hair. "I've just spent the last few days traveling between Denver and Los Angeles setting up a deal."

"I didn't know that, Case. And Mr. Coolidge called again, threatening to—"

"This is all Coolidge is going to need for now." Case stuck his finger onto the manila folder he'd tossed down. "Damn it, Sarah. Why couldn't you have waited? You could have called to let me know what you were planning."

Case fumed, his gaze pinning her down.

"I didn't know when you'd be back or—" Sarah let that thought drop, but it was too late. Far too late.

Realization dawned then, and Case narrowed his dark eyes, his expression thunderous, his body tightening. He growled, low and menacing. "Or *if* I'd be back. Is that it, Sarah? You didn't think I was coming back."

Sarah couldn't meet his eyes. She stared at the folder, then at the floor and back again to the vase on the table.

"That's it. You didn't think I'd be coming back." Case's derisive laughter permeated the room.

"It doesn't matter now," Sarah defended. "I've paid the loan and we're out of debt for the time being."

Case leaned over the table, his palms bracing his weight. "I've signed a contract with Cougar Creek Saddles, doing endorsements for them. Drew Barnett helped put this deal together and I've got an advance check in here to pay off the bank and any other debts we have on the ranch. It's something I'd rather not do. But I did it, Sarah. And do you know why?"

Sarah drew in her lip, shaking her head.

"Because I said I'd get us out of this mess and I meant it." Case began pacing again, his boots scraping the floor so hard he'd wear out the ceramic tile floor before too long. "And what about the night we spent in the barn? We made love, Sarah. If you thought I'd run out on you after *that,* then nothing's changed, has it? It's just too damn bad, nobody around here has any faith in me." He grabbed the portfolio off the table and strode out of the room, leaving Sarah alone with her misery.

She'd misjudged Case terribly on this. He'd spent all this time, setting up a deal to do endorsements for saddles. Case had been asked before, but had solemnly refused, claiming he wasn't a showman or a salesman. He'd always said he wanted to bank on his talent as a horseman and nothing more. He'd made an honorable sacrifice to help the Triple R. The ranch was out of debt now, but Sarah felt she'd just lost something far more valuable. The loss was even more unsettling than giving up her grandmother's emerald ring and the damage done, irreparable.

Because the sad fact remained, Sarah hadn't trusted Case.

And she still didn't know if she ever would.

* * *

Case sat on the front porch, slugging down a beer, watching the cinnamon Arizona sun meet the horizon. The sight, as remarkable and serene as it was, didn't bring solace. Case was in a mood. He couldn't fight it anymore. All he wanted to do was get blissfully, mindlessly drunk.

When the screen door creaked open, Case didn't turn around. ''Supper's on the table,'' Sarah said quietly.

Hell, her sweet flowery scent washed away all the odors of the ranch. How could one little woman obliterate the smell of horse dung, dry red earth and a pasture full of cattle? ''I'm not hungry.''

She'd destroyed his appetite. He didn't think he could spend time with her tonight. The pain of her implied accusation stung too painfully to ignore. She'd thought he'd left her for good. She actually believed he'd abandon her, leaving her to deal with all the ranch problems on her own. How could she think that? Was her regard for him so low? But damn her, they'd made *love*, and it had meant something to him. He'd dreamed of the night he could claim Sarah as his own. But he hadn't, not really, because the hell of it was, she still didn't trust him. And he was spitting mad at himself because he still wanted her.

''Case, please,'' she said softly.

If he looked at her, into those deep blue eyes, she'd melt his resolve. He summoned all his anger, but tempered it with a soft voice. Hurting Sarah had never been his intent. ''I'm fine for now, Sarah. You go on. Have your meal.''

He slugged the last drop of his beer and grabbed another bottle.

''Okay,'' she said, tentatively. He imagined her nibbling on her bottom lip, a habit that fascinated him. ''I'll put your dinner in the fridge for later. Good night, Case.''

Case nodded, his back to her. When the screen door shut softly, Case leaned heavily against the back post and closed his eyes, thinking that military torture techniques would be easier to take than living with Sarah, wanting her so badly that his entire body reacted with need. Knowing that she'd never be his and that she'd never come to trust him was the worst form of torment.

True, in the past he hadn't given her much reason to trust him. He'd been a tease in school, constantly baiting her, at times pretending he was Reid and getting her to say and do things that she normally wouldn't have. Sarah had always fought back, giving as good as she got. He'd always admired that about her, but it hadn't dawned on him until the very last prank that his teasing games might have honestly hurt her. And now the hurt that he'd inflicted as a child had come back to haunt him.

With his eyes still closed, images surged forth of Sarah, looking pretty as a picture in a bright summer dress the day after her junior high school graduation, standing by the creek that ran alongside her grandmother's property. Case had come up behind her, feigning sincerity and handed her a note from Reid that he'd forged. "I'm sorry, Sarah," he'd said. "Reid didn't have the courage to do this himself."

With trembling hands, Sarah read the words that Case had written, stating that Reid wanted to break up with her. He wanted to be free for the summer. Case had expected disbelief, he'd expected outrage, he'd expected for Sarah to march over to the Jarrett house and give Reid a good tongue-lashing. Everybody in town knew Reid was over the moon for Sarah. He thought she'd known it, too. But what he hadn't expected was for Sarah's sweet expression to fall, for her blue eyes to cloud with tears, for her to run away, too fast and furious for Case to stop her.

By the time Case had caught up with her, the damage had already been done. Sarah had cried so hard her eyes looked like two big red swollen puffs on a tearstained face. And when Case owned up to his deception, Sarah had given him a look that cut straight through his heart. With a shaky voice, she'd asked him only one question, why? Why had he done it?

Case had been at a loss. No apologies fell from his lips, nothing to help ease Sarah's pain, but from that day forth Case had vowed he'd never play another prank on Sarah.

And strangely enough, Sarah had never told Reid about it. She hadn't ever wanted to come between the two brothers and she must have been pretty sure of Reid's reaction. He would have throttled Case. Case wouldn't have blamed him. He knew he'd deserved anything Reid had in store for him. But Sarah covered for him, never giving away what Case had done and how much he'd hurt her.

"Damn," he said, popping his eyes open. He looked down at the four bottles of beer he'd yet to drink. "I'll take a rain check," he muttered, jerking his body up from the steps, realizing there was one very important thing Case had to do for Sarah.

Perhaps it would, in a small way, make up for some of the past hurt.

Sarah returned home from a visit with Bobbi Sue the next afternoon to a crowd of hat-waving men standing around the corral, leaning up against the metal fencing. She unlatched Christiana from her car seat and lifted her into her arms. "C'mon, baby girl, let's see what all the fuss is about." She walked over to where Pete was standing by the fence. He turned to her with a big smile. "Howdy, Sarah. How's Baby Jarrett today?"

"Hi Pete. She's just fine." Sarah adjusted her position so Pete could gain a better view of the baby.

"Whoa! That little one's picking up weight faster than a tumbleweed on a windy day."

Sarah chuckled. "That's what the doctor says, too." She turned toward the fence in time to see Case, wearing leather chaps, a Stetson and a pair of work gloves, mount a feisty stallion. "What's going on?"

"Old Bart Winslow bet Case he couldn't break his high-spirited new paint. He brought him over less than an hour ago."

"Really?"

"The dang horse threw him three times already, but Case is giving us all a good show. He's determined to saddle break that piebald today."

Sarah moved closer to the fence, watching the Case Jarrett Rodeo. Case threw his leg over the Association saddle, mounted the horse, all the while keeping a firm grip on the braided buck rein. The horse bucked high, his long legs thrusting up in unison, but Case held on, keeping his balance in classic form. The frustrated bronc continued to buck, moving around the arena, lifting Case high in the air. His last tirade sent Case flying off. His body landed with a thud on the ground. The crowd of ranchers let out moans, shaking their heads and mumbling. Case only smiled, stared at his four-legged opponent then grabbed his hat, ready to mount the horse again.

"Seems he's met his match. That stallion is sure a stubborn one," Pete said. "But Case won't give up. I know that boy and when he wants something bad enough, nothing stops him."

Sarah shuddered. Case had taken a hard fall. She'd

noticed a grimace of pain streak across his face before he'd put on a smile for his audience. "I can't watch this."

Pete grinned. "He's all right, Sarah. No need to worry over him."

"I'm not worried, Pete." But Sarah knew Pete could see straight through her. She *was* worried about Case. She cared for him more than she wanted to admit. She couldn't stand by and watch him punish his body that way. Heck, Case had made a living riding bucking broncos, but she'd never had to witness it before. "I've got to get the baby down for her nap. I'll see you later, Pete."

Another wave of groans from the crowd told Sarah, Case had taken another fall. She dashed into the house and closed the door. "Living with your uncle is a trial I surely wasn't expecting," she whispered to the baby.

Sarah spent the next thirty minutes nursing Christiana and humming a soft lullaby to get her down for her afternoon nap. Christiana loved her naps, thank goodness, and the baby fell right to sleep.

Sarah kissed her softly on the forehead and laid her down in her crib. Tiptoeing out of the room, Sarah bumped into a rock solid chest. "Oh, sorry," she whispered.

Case backed away, his fresh lime scent drifting away with him. "No problem."

Not for him, she thought. Heat shot up her spine from the innocent contact and she knew for certain that unruly hormones had nothing to do with it. Case's presence created a fiery furnace in her body and his touch, the strike of ignition.

"Did you break the stallion?" she asked.

On a modest shrug, he nodded. "Yep. Is Christie asleep?"

"Yes, she's napping."

"Wait right here, Sarah," he said, his voice filled with determination. "I've got something for you."

Sarah stood motionless in stunned silence, waiting, her curiosity peaked. When Case came out of his room a moment later, holding a ring box in his hand, all sorts of strange sensations played havoc with her mind.

But nothing compared to the heart-wrenching emotion Sarah experienced when Case opened the box and handed her grandmother's emerald ring back to her. Tears immediately welled up and her heart pounded hard and furiously against her chest. "Oh, C-Case. I c-can't believe what I'm s-seeing. H-how did you get this?"

"Bobbi Sue gave me some details and I hunted down the jeweler who bought the ring."

"B-but I was just with Bobbi Sue and she didn't mention anything." Sarah's hand trembled as she gazed down at the ring that had been in her family for generations. Her body shook with joy, heartache and myriad emotions she couldn't name.

"I asked her not to say anything."

"I—I, uh, I don't know what to say."

Sarah peered into his eyes then her gaze went to his lips. She wanted to kiss that somber twitch away, to show him how much this meant to her. She wanted his arms around her, the way they'd been the other night when Pretty Girl had had her colt. She wanted more from Case than his brooding eyes would allow.

"Say you'll never get a fool notion in your head again about selling off your ring." Case cast her a stern look.

Tears streamed down freely now. She couldn't hold them back. But her heart swelled with joy. "Okay, I promise."

"Then, that's all there is for you to say."

"Thank you, Case. I could say that, too. It means…it means so much to me."

She clutched the ring to her chest.

Case granted her a quick smile before a frown stole over his face. He glanced down at his right wrist. It was two sizes larger than the other one. "Case! What happened?"

"Nothing. It'll be all right. I landed on it wrong when the stallion threw me. It's just bruised."

Strawberry-red and completely swollen, Sarah doubted Case had merely bruised his wrist. "It doesn't look good, Case. Let me ice it to get the swelling down. Then we can see how bad it is."

Case backed away, shaking his head. "No, thanks. I'll have Pete take a look at it. He can wrap it if he thinks it's necessary."

"O-okay," Sarah said, hesitantly. If Case didn't want her help, she couldn't force the issue. He was still angry with her. "But let me know if you need anything."

He smiled again, another brief lifting of his lips. "I won't." She watched him head down the stairs and a feeling of dire desolation churned in her belly. He didn't want anything to do with her and oddly now, Sarah wanted everything to do with him.

Later that night, Case rested his head on his pillow, stretched out flat on his back on the bed, favoring his right hand. Pete had taped it this afternoon, thinking that after the swelling went down somewhat, the wrist should be immobilized.

He had better things to do than busting stubborn stallions, but the challenge had been made and Case rarely backed down from a challenge. More so, he owed Bart Winslow a favor and though it put his wrist sorely out of commission, he hadn't minded climbing up on that feisty paint. For old time's sake.

His rodeo days were behind him now. He'd made up his mind not to go back. Leaving Sarah and little Christie just wasn't in the cards. He *wanted* to settle down, stay on the ranch and make a go of it, with the two of them by his side. He wanted roots again. He was through ambling from town to town, competing during the day and engaging in rowdy rodeo antics at night. None of that mattered now.

He wanted the family that he, Sarah and Christie seemed to portray to the world.

He wanted Sarah for his own.

Wanting and getting were two entirely different matters.

Hell, he was still smarting from Sarah's lack of faith in him. He hated the thought that she'd never change her mind about him, no matter what he did, or how he tried to prove otherwise. Sarah would always look upon him as the bad seed, the brother who had abandoned the ranch when he had been most needed. She'd always see him as the man who had played one too many hurtful pranks on her.

The truth of it was, Case really believed Sarah had deep down, honest, feelings for him. When they'd made love, she'd responded with fiery passion and sizzling heat.

There was no denying that they had a connection, an electrifying spark that left them both yearning for more. He knew Sarah wasn't the type of woman to make love to a man without genuine feelings. She'd said she'd needed him, and he understood that, but she'd wanted him, too. She'd told him with every female sigh, every arch of her willing body and every whimper of pleasure that she'd wanted him as much as he did her.

Yet, she wouldn't allow her feelings to surface. She wouldn't see him for the man that he was. Case couldn't abide by that. He was through trying. This was one challenge he wouldn't take on, because the pain of losing would make living here, under the same roof with Sarah, far too hard to bear. He'd pretty much reconciled himself to life on the ranch, watching out for Sarah and the baby, loving them in distant silence and most important, keeping the vow he'd made to his brother. With decided resignation, Case closed his eyes and hoped welcomed peace would claim him.

Little Christie's cries from the nursery put a smile on his face. Case rose from the bed, slipping on his jeans with his left hand and walked into the nursery. Dim yellow hues created by an angel cherub night-light cast the room in a dewy glow. "Hello, little beauty," he said, bending over the crib.

Christie stopped crying the minute she saw him, giving him a bright-eyed look that warmed his heart. At least, this female appreciated the love he had to offer. And he wouldn't let her down. Not ever.

Case picked her up. "Want to rock a bit?" he whispered, taking her up in his left arm then moving to the rocker. "We'll let your mama sleep."

Christie cuddled close to his chest, grabbing at his hairs, making him cringe from the tight grasp she had on him. "Easy now," he said with pride, uncurling her fingers a bit. "There, that's better." Jarretts were strong and even this little one displayed her strength with powerful hair-tugging hands.

Case began humming a cowboy tune they used to sing

around the campfires at night. He didn't know any lull-abies.

"Hi," Sarah whispered, coming into the room. She wore an oversize white T-shirt, that landed somewhere just above her knees. Glimmering light cast her in silhouette, her form outlined by the soft radiance. Case stopped humming and swallowed hard, noting the contours, the pebbled peaks lifting the shirt up higher in front than in back. There was slight moisture there, just a hint of it, but enough for Case to know, Sarah was ready to nurse the baby. "I guess she's not going to sleep through tonight. I didn't hear her, but woke just a minute ago and came to check on her. Did she cry?"

It hurt to look at Sarah, to know the life they could have, if only she'd allow it. Anger and pain surfaced again taking hold of him. "She cried."

Sarah stood above him, watching him snuggle with the baby. Awkward silence ensued. Sarah shifted her stance and Case tried damn hard not to notice the sway of material, the way it pushed tight against her breasts. Damn hard. Problem was, he couldn't forget touching her there, his hands roving over each swell, his body growing harder each time she moaned from the pleasure.

"I can take her," she offered, reaching her arms out. "I, uh, need to feed her."

Carefully Case rose from the rocker. He handed the baby over to her. Instantly she noticed his wrapped wrist. "How's the injury?"

He shrugged. "I'll live."

Sarah nibbled on her lower lip and nodded, those blue eyes filled with hesitation. "Thanks for getting up for her."

"No thanks necessary. She's my niece."

"I know, but I don't expect you to—"

"Christie is my flesh and blood, Sarah. I love her. You're just going to have to get used to that."

Case strode out of the room before he said any more. He'd been harsh and cold and every cell in his body screamed Jerk, Jerk, Jerk. Yet, it was his only defense, holding on to his anger and pain was the only way he knew to protect himself, to keep from falling any harder for Sarah.

# Ten

"**D**amn it!"

Sarah heard Case's oath from her bedroom. He'd cursed three times in as many minutes. Although he'd been in a sour mood lately, he hid his ornery disposition with infuriating politeness. Yet, Sarah knew, Case had been stung by her mistrust and after pondering it for a time she'd come to the conclusion that she owed the man a deep apology.

He'd come through in a big way, but Sarah hadn't given him an ounce of her faith. She'd believed him capable of abandoning her, the baby and the ranch. Yet, he'd not only proven that he'd been capable of fixing their monetary problems, he'd returned her grandmother's ring. It was by far the sweetest, most sincere gesture she'd ever received from him.

Yes, she owed him one heartfelt apology. It wouldn't come easy. She'd been putting it off for days, hoping to see a glimmer of the easygoing Case she knew him to be. But that Case had all but disappeared from the Triple R and she feared it was all due to her.

"Ah, hell!" His low raspy curse rattled her nerves.

On impulse, Sarah wandered toward his room, but instead, found him in the bathroom just off the hallway.

"Case?" She peeked inside the doorway and squinted against the early morning sun streaming through the curtains.

He turned to her, his face a patchwork of tiny tissues dotted with red blood. His blood. The man had been trying to shave with a bandaged and very sore wrist.

"What is it, Sarah?"

His frown was enough to back her up a step. "Uh, I heard you in here. Can I help?"

"No, I'm doing just fine."

He wasn't doing fine. He'd barely managed to scrap off one layer of his three-day growth of beard and there was more blood on his face than shaving cream.

"You're not doing just fine, Case Jarrett, and don't try to bulldoze me. You're bleeding all over the place."

"Well, shoot, Sarah. I can't get the right angle with my wrist hog-tied like it is."

"I know," she offered softly, taking a look at his bandaged wrist. "Have a seat and let me shave your beard."

He pointed his finger. "You?" Dark eyes narrowed on her. "You know what you're doing?"

"Scared?"

His lips curved up slightly, a crooked smile erupting. Sarah realized she'd missed those smiles in the past few days. "Yep."

"Good, now take a seat." She gave him a little shove toward the bathtub rim and he plopped down, his brows arched and his expression, curious. "And watch me work.'' She handed him a moistened towel to wipe off the remnants of shave cream from his face.

''I don't know, Sarah…'' he began, juggling the towel in his fist, ''putting a sharp razor in your hand and coming at my throat. If you'd wanted revenge—''

''For hiding all of Snowball's kittens and telling me she'd *eaten* them.''

His lips twitched. ''You were nine. I didn't really think you'd believe me.''

''I was eight and I didn't, but I didn't know what you'd done with them, either.''

His tone became defensive. ''I wouldn't have hurt them. They were cute. And I gave them back that same afternoon.''

''Hmm. And how about when I was in the seventh grade and you dumped water down my blouse right before I had to give my report on the Civil War?''

Case outwardly cringed, his expression filled with regret. ''Can I apologize now, for that one?''

Sarah lifted the razor from the tile counter. ''I worked the entire weekend on that report.''

Case eyed her warily. ''You must've hated me.''

Sarah hesitated, thinking back. ''I didn't really.'' And that was the truth. Case had teased and played tricks on her, but Sarah hadn't hated him. She didn't have hate in her heart for anyone, either now or then. But, she'd never trusted him and had learned early on to never believe a word he'd said. Those habits died hard. Yet, Sarah found herself fumbling for a way to apologize to him. He'd done a good thing this time, and he deserved her apology.

Sarah shook the can of shave cream, pressed the nozzle and let the snowy lime-scented cream flow into her hand. Case watched her, then after a moment, wiped his face clean with the towel in his hand.

"That's what I liked best about you, Sarah. You never went crying home to Mama. You never wilted away. I admired that about you. Your strength."

"I didn't think you liked me at all."

Case inhaled, eyeing her now, from the top of her ponytail down to her leather boots, not missing anything in between. Case had a way of looking at a woman, at *her,* that made her feel soft and feminine and desirable.

He sat there perusing her, looking mighty desirable himself, wearing faded jeans and a sleeveless tank that exposed a fair amount of tanned muscle. And when he spoke quietly in a husky voice, Sarah's bones nearly melted. "I liked you, Sarah."

She nodded, a lump forming in her throat. She'd better get her apology out before she wasn't able to speak at all. "I'm sorry, Case."

He shifted uncomfortably and raised his voice a bit. "That I liked you?"

"No, no." Sarah let out a nervous chuckle. Lamely she tried to explain. "I meant to say…I've been meaning to say, well, I apologize for not believing you the other day. You got the money we needed, just like you said you would. I, uh, I guess I should have had more faith in you."

Case didn't say anything. She was certain she'd shocked him. He sat there, dark eyes wide, staring at her. Was he still angry with her?

"Will you forgive me?"

Case blinked, then his gaze softened and he lifted his lips in a small smile. "Yeah, Sarah. No problem."

Encouraged, Sarah finished her apology. "Returning my grandmother's ring was…the sweetest thing in this world."

Case couldn't believe he'd heard right. Sarah apologized to him. She'd thought he'd done something *sweet*. If that didn't beat all.

Case never thought he'd hear Sarah admit she'd been wrong about him. Well, she hadn't been wrong in the past. He could acknowledge that now. He'd been hurtful toward her and he'd be forever sorry about that, but maybe Sarah was beginning to see him differently now. Maybe she could forget the past and begin to see him for the man he was today. "That ring will belong to Christie one day, Sarah. No matter what happens on the ranch, you keep that ring."

"I will." She took a moment to exhale.

"Good," he said, right before Sarah's hand came up to spread shave cream all over his face. Her touch, the soft way she rubbed her fingers through his beard, put notions in his head, of other things she could do with those hands. She stood close, between his legs and her flowery scent penetrated his nostrils. With task at hand now, Sarah concentrated on shaving him.

Ah hell, he thought, as his entire body went tight from watching her perform the simple act. He had a great view, a *first-class* view of Sarah's ample cleavage and was having a dickens of a time trying to keep from focusing there. After a time, he gave up. Sarah was intent on taking her time, stroking his face with utmost care to notice where his gaze wandered, so he treated himself to her. All of her, up close and wanting to get more personal.

She smelled so damn good. And every so often, she'd rest a hand on his shoulder for balance, or she'd meet his eyes briefly and smile. Once when she turned to rinse the razor, her breast rubbed against his arm. She hadn't noticed, or if she had, she'd pretended she hadn't felt anything. But for Case, there was no pretending away the soft swell brushing against him, teasing him, tempting him, far beyond his limit.

Case didn't know such torment existed. He wanted to hold her again and kiss her senseless. Hell, he wanted to toss that razor out and set her on his lap, make love to her that way.

Case's mind flashed hot erotic images of the different ways he'd like to make love to Sarah. He knew how she would respond now. Sarah had a passionate nature. He'd been lucky enough to make love to her once and just thinking about that night got him overheated. Moisture pooled on his brow. If Sarah noticed, he'd blame it on Arizona heat, but it was her heat and the intensity of his feelings for her, causing him to break out in a sweat.

"There, just about through," she said. "Wasn't that painless?"

He grunted his thanks. It was getting sizzling hot in the bathroom. And she thought that was *painless?* Being tossed off Dynamite Dan, one rowdy stallion had been less painful than having Sarah so close.

She took a towel and wiped off his face, then peered at his scar. With a finger, she traced the rough edges that slanted down from his right eye. The soft caress, the trail of her fingers on his face, left him yearning for more. Her touch sharpened everything male inside. "This must have hurt."

"It hurts more looking at you," he said honestly, offering no further explanation.

Sarah's eyes grew wide. "Don't say those things, Case."

Her breathy voice did something to him. It was about all he could take. He stood and drew her into his arms, splaying his hands around her slimmed down waist. He brought her up close with a gentle tug, his hips meeting with her belly. Sarah gasped her surprise at his bold move, but didn't back away, and the contact, their connection was pure heaven. He lowered his head. "I think you know what I mean, Sarah. But I'm going to show you anyway."

His lips were sizzling hot, his kiss sweetly gentle. The combination sent ripples of excitement through Sarah's body. Case took his time, slanting his mouth over hers with exquisite tenderness. He tilted his head, licked at her lips, murmured something soft and sweet then claimed her mouth again. Sarah moaned softly from the delicious sensation. Case Jarrett sure knew how to kiss a woman. He always had.

He cupped her face with his good hand and spread his fingers through her hair, tilting her head up. Their eyes met briefly before she closed hers again, but the look in his eyes, the urgency and need couldn't be denied. This time, his lips crushed hers with heat, a passion Sarah was just beginning to understand. She met his passion with her own, a crazy intense blending of lips that demanded more.

Case parted her lips and their tongues entwined, mating together as if they'd been preordained. A deep groan of pleasure escaped his throat and Sarah rejoiced at the heady sound. He kissed her again and again, his breaths as rapid and labored as hers.

"Sarah," he said, a raspy whisper of need, "come here." He sat down and took her with him. She landed on his lap and wrapped her arms around his neck, the scent of lime and fresh soap enveloping her.

Sarah's head spun. She was certain she was out of her mind especially after what happened between them the other night, but she hadn't the will or the power to stop this wildness. And when he nudged her closer, the full extent of his desire pressed against her, Sarah lost all rational thought.

Case kissed her again, his mouth gentle at times, bruising at others. His lips traveled down her throat, playing close and dangerous with the edge of her cherry red tank top. He stopped then, cast her a heated look, smiled, then with slow calculation, he lowered the straps of both her bra and her top. She felt the cool morning air hit her chest.

"So beautiful, Sarah."

Sarah's heart pumped with such fierceness she thought it would burst from her chest. And when Case lowered his mouth to graze one fully aroused peak with his tongue, she flung her head back and cried out, both pleasured and tortured at the same time. *"Ohhh."*

Spirals of heat climbed up her from her belly as Case kissed her with finesse, stroked her with sure hands and left her wild with want. "Case?"

"I can't get enough of you, lady," he whispered with velvety smoothness.

His words seared straight through her. The truth was, she couldn't seem to get enough of him, either. And that scared her more than anything else ever had because she still didn't trust him. She couldn't wipe away the last twenty years so easily. She'd known Case before, but how well did she know him now? She wanted him, but she still had little faith in him. What did that say about her? About him? Confusion warred with desire, but the decision was instantly taken out of her hands. The phone rang.

"I'll get it," she said, attempting to lift up from Case's lap.

He smiled and pulled her back down. "Let it ring, sweetheart."

She hesitated, listening to the ringing. Then, the baby cried. And cried and cried.

When she looked at Case, he sighed with resignation. "I'll get the phone," he muttered on an agonized groan, "soon as I can stand again."

"And I'll get the baby," she said, righting the straps of her top and backing out of the bathroom. There were some major advantages to being female, Sarah decided, as she headed to the nursery.

Case yanked the phone from its socket. "Hello," he grumbled.

"Whoa! Did I get you out of bed or something?"

The *or something* would have landed him in bed, with Sarah, if the darn phone hadn't interrupted. Case's body still hummed from their all-too-brief encounter in the bathroom. "Hello, Carl."

"Case, are you ready for some bad news?"

"It's been that kind of morning. What's up?"

"There's been trouble at Keith Dryer's farm. Seems somebody got into the house while the Dryers were away. Everything was turned upside down. Made a big mess of things inside, but nothing was stolen. The sheriff came out to investigate. Seems the Beckman Corporation is denying any part in this. But, they'd sent an agent over to their house not five days earlier, trying to get them to sell."

Case absorbed the information as doubts crept in. Even though an agent had come out to badger Sarah about selling, Case wondered if such a high-powered corporation would stoop to such low levels, committing crimes, risking their business, in order to get what they wanted.

Intimidation in the form of high-handed land agents was one thing, but the actual commission of crimes, was certainly another. "Seems a bit too convenient, doesn't it?"

Carl agreed. "That's what I was thinking. For a while there, I thought those Beckman agents were behind everything happening around here. Now, I'm not so sure. Hardly seems like the doings of a company on the New York Stock Exchange."

"Yeah, I'm starting to see it that way, too. But none of it makes a darn bit of sense. And you say, nothing was stolen from Keith's house, so what's the point, other than to frighten and intimidate the landowners in Barrel Springs?" Case decided that he wasn't going to let Christiana and Sarah out of his sight from now on.

Carl added, "Three of our neighbors have sold their places, but the rest of us are hanging on. It doesn't look good for those Bridle Path Homes, right about now."

"Yeah, I was hoping they'd cut their losses, pack up and leave us all alone."

"Maybe they will if they don't get enough of us to sell out. They'll end up with a miniature golf course instead of a five-star championship green."

"Yeah, and pony rides, instead of state-of-the-art stables. Now, that would be worth seeing."

Carl laughed, his deep voice going soft and smooth. "Seems like Bobbi Sue and me are going to have something worth seeing in about eight more months, ourselves."

Case's mind grabbed hold of that, realizing what Carl meant. "No kidding? You're going to have a baby?"

"Yeah, little Mo's beside herself, hoping for a baby sister, but don't spill the beans to Sarah. Bobbi Sue wants to tell her herself."

"Damn, Carl. That's great. Congratulations. And I won't let on to Sarah."

"Okay, just have Sarah call her today. Bobbi Sue's ready to burst with the news, but she didn't want to call too early. And you watch out for that little family of yours over there, too. No telling what's going to happen next."

Case hung up with Carl with two niggling thoughts in mind. Whether Sarah would agree or not that they were a little family, as Carl put it, and the fact that Case wouldn't allow any harm to come to any of them. He wouldn't let anyone destroy the ranch and all that his brother Reid had worked so hard to attain. He wouldn't let anyone frighten Sarah again, or put her in danger. He'd protect Sarah and Christie with his life.

And then there was Carl's announcement. Case had never given much thought to kids, wanting them, having them, becoming a father himself, until he came to live here again. Now, Case found himself envious of Carl, wanting so much to be a father to little Christie, and wanting to have children with Sarah. Hell, the thought scared the stuffing out of him, but at the same time, put a wide smile on his face. Having Sarah's children? He couldn't ask for anything more.

Case strode down the hall and stood outside the nursery watching Sarah finish dressing the baby in a pale pink dress with bloomers twice her size. "There now, sweet girl, don't you look pretty?"

"She does," Case said, entering the room. "Right down to her cute pink booties."

Sarah laughed, picking the baby up, but she didn't look at him. In fact, she looked everywhere, but at him. Case let out a silent sigh of resignation. After that night in the barn, he understood that Sarah was running scared. Case hoped it wasn't so, but he knew Sarah all too well.

"That was Carl on the phone. Seems, there was another incident. Keith Dryer's place was broken into."

Case went on to explain the circumstances while Sarah made herself busy with Christie. "I want you to be careful, Sarah. No telling what might happen next."

"I will be," she said, nodding, putting Christie in the crook of her arm and bouncing her gently on her hip. Her gaze focused solely on the baby.

"Sarah?" Case stepped closer. He wanted Sarah to admit that something special was happening between them. Something unique, rare and okay, maybe a bit complicated, but hell, good things didn't always come too easy.

She lifted her head up, finally meeting his eyes. "You said Bobbi Sue wants to speak with me? I'd better call her. Here," she said, handing Christie over to him, her expression so guarded, Case wanted to punch the wall. Just minutes ago, she'd let down her guard with him and it had nearly knocked him to his knees. "Will you take her for a few minutes?"

"Sure, darlin'. I'd never refuse little Christie."

"Okay," she said, her relief apparent. "I'll, uh, go call Bobbi Sue."

Case nestled Christie in his left arm and called to Sarah, just as she walked out of the nursery, "You can't keep running from me, Sarah."

She stopped, hesitated, but didn't turn to face him. "I'm...not...running, Case." Then she dashed down the hallway.

Running.

# Eleven

Sarah ushered Bobbi Sue, Carl and little Maureen into the house then quickly hugged her best friend. "I'm so happy for you, Bobbi Sue. This is wonderful news." Sarah turned to Carl and kissed his cheek. "Congratulations."

"I'm gonna be the big sister," little Maureen offered in earnest.

Sarah bent down and hugged her tight. "Yes, and you'll be the best sister ever. I just know it, sweetheart."

Sarah brought her guests into the kitchen where dinner was just about ready. She'd invited them over tonight on impulse, overjoyed at Bobbi Sue's news, but also grateful to have an excuse not to be alone with Case tonight. She'd been doing that lately whenever she could, finding ways not to be alone with him. Her sister, Delaney's visit acted as a buffer and now, her dear friends had come to the rescue.

Only Sarah wasn't entirely sure she needed rescuing. What she needed was time to sort out her feelings. She'd spent the last weeks in a state of confusion where Case was concerned, and no doubt why. Her life had taken more turns in the past year than she could ever have imagined. *Never* in her wildest of dreams, would she have thought that she'd have feelings—real, honest, heartfelt feelings for Case Jarrett. She'd been fighting them off, unsure of him, unsure of herself.

Yet, Case wasn't a man to be ignored.

That fact became even more evident when he walked into the room, wearing a smile for their guests, dressed in a clean, chambray shirt pushed up to his elbows, the scent of lime wafting in the air. After that erotic shave this morning, Sarah would never think on that innocent scent as anything but magnetic, drawing her in, reminding her of the appealing man who had nearly toppled all of her defenses.

Case greeted their friends and they all sat down to eat pot roast, creamed corn, roasted potatoes and biscuits. Everyone ate up heartily, except for Bobbi Sue.

"Are you having morning sickness?" Sarah asked, after the meal. The men had taken Maureen out to see Striker, the new colt.

"Not really. Just a bit queasy at times." Bobbi Sue put a hand on her stomach.

"It won't last long, hopefully. I got over my morning sickness in the third month. Then the pregnancy was a breeze."

"I know. I remember, sort of. Five years is a long time. Carl and I, well, we didn't really plan this," Bobbi Sue confided.

"No?"

She chuckled and shook her head. "No, in fact, the

news was enough to put a shock in both of us. But now, we couldn't be happier. Just took some time getting used to the idea.''

Sarah grinned. ''It'll be great for Christiana to have a baby to play with. They won't be too far away in age. The new baby and little Mo will be the closest she'll have to real siblings.'' Sarah sighed deeply, a melancholy mood settling in. ''Sometimes, I wish she didn't have to be an only child. I don't know what I would have done without Delaney growing up. Of course, we didn't have a usual childhood. But then, Christiana won't, either.''

''Sure she will, honey. She's got you and you're a terrific mother. And Case, well, anybody can see how much that man adores that child.''

Somehow the conversation always came back to Case. Sarah didn't want to bank on him. She didn't know when or if he'd leave the ranch, no matter his claims otherwise. She'd been hurt in the past, terribly, losing Reid, the father of her child. She couldn't afford to rely on a man she couldn't really trust. If she did, and he left again, Sarah's heart would shatter all over again. She didn't know if she could take that. ''Case is a great uncle to Christiana. But—''

''But?'' Bobbi Sue listened intently.

''But, I just don't know him well enough to…I mean to say, what if Christiana becomes attached to him and then he packs up and leaves us?''

Bobbi Sue thought on that a minute, casting Sarah a long penetrating look. ''Sarah, the way I see it, the only way that man is going to leave this ranch is if you drive him away. I'm telling you, he's staying this time. Carl tells me Case has got all kinds of plans for the ranch. He really wants to make a go of it. You need to give him a chance, honey. Let him prove himself.''

"I'm just trying to protect my daughter." And myself, she didn't add. As yet, she hadn't confided in Bobbi Sue about her encounters with Case. About the way she was beginning to feel about him, despite her worries. She hadn't shared that information with anyone.

Bobbi Sue smiled. "You're a good mother. I can understand you worrying over her. Let's face it, Case does have a reputation to live down. But, I think he's trying, Sarah."

"Mmm, maybe." Sarah just couldn't be sure and there was far too much at risk to make a mistake.

Little Mo came barreling back inside, her face awash with joy. Case and Carl were just steps behind her. "Uncle Case says I can ride Striker when he gets a mite older!"

"That's great, honey," Bobbi Sue said, stroking her daughter's hair. "Uncle Case will let you know when the colt is old enough to take on a rider."

"And he says it's time for dessert. What's for dessert, Aunt Sarah?"

Sarah blasted Case with a look. He knew darn well her cherry cobbler had flopped. Her mind hadn't been on baking this afternoon. It had been on him and the erotic shave in the bathroom. Every time Case came close, her mind went numb to everything else. Thoughts of him took hold and threatened her sanity as she recalled the power of his touch and the impact of his kiss. Her insides churned with a need Sarah tried real hard to brush aside. But this afternoon Case had wandered in the kitchen just in time to find Sarah biting back a curse when her masterpiece had all but crumbled apart. "Uh, well," Sarah fumbled.

Case's face lit with amusement. "Why don't you look in the refrigerator, Mo?"

Maureen thrust the refrigerator door open. "Wow! Chocolate cake!" With the care only a five-year-old could muster, Maureen lifted the double fudge chocolate cake off the shelf. Her hands wobbled, but she managed to bring the cake safely to the table.

Case winked, bent down and whispered in Sarah's ear. "I picked it up this afternoon."

His warm breath sent shivers down her spine. Case Jarrett was full of surprises. She never knew what he was about to do. That thought thrilled her, but also frightened her. The man was so doggone unpredictable. But at least her guests could plunge into a decadent double-decker chocolate dessert.

Even Bobbi Sue dug in. The room became quiet as they all forked their way through and drank their coffee. And afterward, Case and Sarah walked their guests out to their car. Bobbi Sue and Sarah met with an easy embrace, and Case shook Carl's hand once more as they said their farewells.

Case and Sarah watched the Blazer kick up spirals of red dust down the road before they turned toward the house. Case hesitated on the steps. "I think I'll check on the animals before turning in. See how Pretty Girl and Striker are doing. Want to join me?"

Slowly Sarah shook her head. The last thing she wanted right now was to be alone with Case in the barn. Thoughts rushed in of the night they'd made love. He'd been a wonderful lover; patient and tender with her, a new mother. Decidedly, she needed time to sort out her feelings. Case was just too darn appealing with those quick killer smiles and dark piercing eyes for Sarah to trust herself with him, just yet. Having him near, pretty much clouded all her well-intentioned reasoning. "No thanks. I'm tired. I think I'll put the baby down and get to bed early.''

Eyes twinkling, Case nodded. ''Okay. The meal was real delicious, darlin'.''

Sarah blushed and called herself a silly fool, for acting like an awestruck teenager. ''Thanks.''

Case leaned in and kissed her soundly on the lips. There were no bodies brushing, or arms entwined, or even earth-moving heat this time, just his lips quickly on hers. But the gesture, the familiar, domestic, possessive ritual that happens between a man and his woman, caught her completely off guard.

''Good night, Sarah.''

''G-good night, C-Case.''

Familiar. Domestic. Possessive. Those powerful words made blood rush to Sarah's head. She watched Case walk away, the sexy saunter of a man comfortable in his own skin and so very sure of himself.

She made her way up the steps, certain of one thing only.

She was more uncertain than ever.

Sarah threw her arms into a pale peach, nursing night-gown. The garment was designed with a low swooping neckline to make feeding the baby easier. She'd received the thoughtful gift at her baby shower and was making great use of it. Just as she lowered the sheets down to climb into bed, she heard Case calling out. Low, muted, and filled with dire urgency, his voice jolted straight through her. Sarah donned her silk robe, opened the door, and gasped in horror. Case stood in her doorway, bat-tered, bruised and nearly incoherent.

''Case!''

He leaned against the doorway and dread seized her

instantly when she realized the door frame was all that held him up. "Sarah, you okay? The baby?"

"Yes, yes, we're fine." He leaned forward and his weight fell onto her. She braced herself as his six-foot frame nearly toppled her. "Hold on to me, Case. Let's get you to the bed."

Slowly they moved to her bed, his weight nearly crushing her. But the bed wasn't far and once he'd gotten close, he let her go and allowed his limp body to fall onto the bed. He rolled onto his back and closed his eyes.

"What happened?" Sarah attempted to keep panic out of her voice, but fear rose up instantly seeing Case so badly beaten. Her heart ached just looking at his bloody face and shredded shirt. Was there a lump on his head?

"Don't know exactly. Went into the barn to feed the animals. I was blindsided. Didn't see him coming, I guess. Put up a decent fight, but then I think I got a shovel to my head."

Tears stung Sarah's eyes. "Someone attacked you. Oh, Case. We've got to get a doctor out here."

Case opened his eyes and took great effort to shake his head. "No. I'll be fine, darlin'."

"You could have a concussion."

"I *know* I do. But I've had 'em before and I know what to do. I just need some patching up. What we have to do is call the sheriff. Would you do that, darlin'? Get the sheriff out here."

"Are you sure about the doctor, Case?" Sarah worried her lip, fearful Case needed more medical attention than he claimed he did.

"I'm sure. Just call the sheriff."

The next hour flew by as Sarah administered to Case's wounds, gave Sheriff Pickley her statement after Case had given his, then offered the lawman a cup of coffee.

He sat in her kitchen, sipping slowly, and Sarah cursed her own hospitality. All she wanted to do was get back upstairs to check on Case again.

"Thanks for the coffee, Mrs. Jarrett. I'll get in touch with you if we find out anything." Sheriff Pickley jammed his hat back on his head. "At least this time, we have a vague description. Mr. Jarrett caught a glimpse of the man before he was knocked out."

"I hope you find out who's terrifying the neighbors, Sheriff. The sooner, the better," Sarah added, letting the man out. She dashed up the stairs, peeked in on her sleeping daughter then entered her room.

Case opened his eyes. "Sheriff gone?"

"Yes," she said on a shaky sigh. She nudged her body down next to Case on the bed and dipped a wash towel into a bowl of water. "I'm going to try to keep the swelling down." With caution, she dabbed his face, chin and neck gently.

"Can you help get my shirt off?" he asked softly, "I think one or two ribs are bruised."

The chambray shirt was ripped in several places, but Sarah still took the time to unbutton his shirt and carefully pull the material away from his shoulders. A grimace stole over his face as he sat up slightly to help her remove the garment.

Once done, Sarah bore witness to the three nasty bruise marks on his chest, the color reminding her of overripe plums. "Oh, that looks like it hurts. Are you sure your ribs aren't broken?"

"I wouldn't be breathing easy if they were," he said, granting her a quick smile. What he had to smile about, she didn't know. His body had taken a terrible beating. But Case was strong, and he'd had his share of bruises as a rodeo rider. She banked on his knowledge of injuries. If he were sure then she wouldn't doubt his judgment.

"Tell me if this hurts," she said, "I'm going to clean the wounds. There's some blood on your chest."

With utmost care, Sarah wiped at the blood, fearful of causing Case any more pain.

"You have a gentle touch, Sarah. Don't be afraid."

"I can't stand to see you hurt," she blurted out.

Case's dark eyes softened. "I'll be fine, darlin'. Don't worry."

"What about your head? There's a lump the size of Phoenix erupting on your scalp."

"It's not as bad as it looks."

"But, if it is a concussion, doesn't that mean that you shouldn't sleep tonight? I mean…well, someone should watch over you, right?"

"Usually, if there's someone willing." Was he hinting? She wondered if Case wanted her to sleep next to him tonight to look after him. And what of it? He'd been badly beaten protecting her, the baby and the Triple R. She owed him her help and she doubted she'd get any sleep anyway tonight worrying about him. She admonished herself for her crazy notions. The handsome cowboy was simply too banged up to have thoughts of lust, when it was plain to see he could barely keep his eyes open.

"I'm willing…to help you. Of course, I'll watch over you tonight."

"Thank you, Sarah. You must be tired. Why don't you lie down? Keep me company."

Sarah hesitated then thought she'd gone completely loco. Case could barely move a muscle. He needed her friendship tonight, nothing more. The man had a concussion, after all.

"Okay." She set the bowl and towels aside then slid down next to him on the bed. She whispered, "What do I do, if you start to fall asleep?"

A chuckle rumbled from his chest. "Sarah, honey, there are a dozen and a half things you can do to keep me awake."

Sarah wanted to swat him, but she didn't dare for fear of causing him more injury. The man had an *ego* the size of Phoenix, matching the lump on his head. "Honestly, Case. Is that all that's ever on your mind?"

"You want honesty, Sarah? Only since I've been living with you."

*Only since I've been living with you.*

Sarah's heart tripped over itself. He sounded so sincere, so earnest and she wondered if he really meant it. Case had been attracted to her, but was it more than that? Did he have genuine feelings for her?

Sarah still had trouble believing in him, so she changed the subject and they talked for a while. Well, she did most of the talking and Case, most of the listening. He seemed alert, as she spouted off about the rising cost of grain, Bobbi Sue's pregnancy, how fast Christiana seemed to be growing. She spoke of anything and everything, and Case nodded occasionally, added his opinions a few times and laughed with her when she'd relay one of her baby daughter's newest antics.

It seemed as natural as breathing when Case's hand entwined with hers, lacing their fingers. He held fast and firm, needing to feel the connection, she presumed, but the contact made her feel things, too. She lay in bed with him, worrying over his injuries, trying to entertain him, and hoping that he wouldn't have a bad night.

An hour later, Sarah realized she'd dozed off. When she opened her eyes, Case, too, seemed to be sleeping.

She debated whether to let him rest, or wake him. How bad was his concussion? Sarah lifted up a bit to peer at him. He was sleeping soundly, perhaps too soundly. Fear engulfed her and she moved closer to take a better look. ''Case?''

A soft glow of moonlight streaming into the room cast his face in shadows, but there was just enough light to see when his eyes opened. ''Mmm, Sarah, am I dreaming?'' He rolled to his side and faced her, placing a hand on her hip.

''You fell asleep,'' she whispered, fully aware of Case now. He was in sexy sleep-hazy mode, wearing nothing but his jeans and a dynamite smile.

''I'd get beat up every day, if it meant waking up next to you every night.''

A nervous chuckle erupted. ''You don't mean that.''

''I do,'' he said in a husky voice. ''How are you planning on keeping me awake, darlin'?''

Case ran his hand from her hip, down her thigh and back. Even through the material of her robe, she felt his heat, the strength in his hands. Goose bumps broke out on her legs, all the way down and her mind flashed an image of the last time they lay together, when Sarah practically begged him to make love to her. ''Oh, um,'' she tried, but words failed her.

''Kiss me, Sarah,'' he whispered quietly, but his words echoed loudly in her head.

''Case,'' she breathed out and conjured up the first lucid thought in her brain, ''your lips are bruised.''

''That's why I need you.'' His soft gaze locked on to hers and beckoned with honest appeal. Heavens, if she was really truthful with herself she'd admit his entire body called to hers, his need, powerful. An electric spark sizzled between them. Sarah had precious little resistance to such potency.

She brought her lips to his, brushing a soft kiss to his mouth.

"I feel better already, sweetheart." His hand moved over her thigh again, stroking her gently again. They kissed again, and again, each kiss leaving Sarah wanting more. Case undid the tie on her robe and it fell open. The sheer gown she had on underneath did little to conceal her from Case's direct perusal. He saw through the material, perhaps even further, into her heart, which was open and ready to give to him.

He touched her again, his hand slipping up under the soft gossamer of her gown. He teased her with kisses and tempted her with caresses that came dangerously close to making her lose all control. "I want you, Sarah," he confessed, as he parted her legs slightly to define his declaration.

Heat curled her toes, and Sarah slammed her eyes shut. Heaven help her, but she wanted him, too. There was no power on this earth that would take her from this place right now, no thoughts that would break through her desire.

Sarah sat up slightly and removed her robe, then lowered her nightgown down, her answer clear. Case swore, an almost silent oath that told Sarah she was beautiful to him.

Case stared at Sarah in disbelief. Something special *was* happening between them. For Case, it seemed, it had always been so. Years of yearning, nights of wanting, days of denying his desire for her, his brother's wife. But it wasn't enough, he thought with wry irony. They lay here, in the bed she'd shared with Reid, in the house they'd lived in, with Reid's daughter sleeping in the next room and it wasn't enough that Sarah had come to him. He had to be sure he wasn't a replacement for Reid, a trick of Sarah's imagination, lying next to a man who looked identical to her deceased husband. The last time they'd made love, it had been different. Sarah had been desperate for reassurances. She'd been distraught and scared and she'd needed Case. Now it was more, he hoped, but Case had to know for sure. "Say it, Sarah. Say you want me."

Sarah blinked, her expression one of doubt, as if to say wasn't it enough that she was here with him, baring herself to him. He saw the indecision on her face, for only a moment, and then the words came, soft and sweet. Words Case had waited nearly a lifetime to hear. "I want you, Case."

Case kissed her then, passion erupting as he found ways to bring Sarah to deep pleasure, with his hands, his lips, the sway of his body. He kissed her long and hard and nuzzled his face in her hair, breathing her in, taking what she offered with all the greed of a starving man. Clothes parted, sheets tangled and the bed creaked with quiet rebellion as their bodies blended beautifully.

"Case," she called out when she was ready for him and all doubts of where Sarah's mind and heart really were, shattered, bringing him an immense sense of joy.

He rolled onto his back, lifting Sarah with him and let her set the pace. She rose above him, the intoxicating picture she made, permanently imprinted in his mind, as he grasped her hips, guiding her down onto him.

Sarah moved slowly, her face flushed, her eyes closed. She adjusted to him, rising up then down, setting an erotic rhythm. Case gritted his teeth, holding back, seeing to Sarah's pleasure as her muscles tightened around him. She drove him crazy, to the brink and back, a dozen times and Case wouldn't have it any other way. He watched her face change expression, followed her beat, the essence that was Sarah and mated with it, with her, until he knew the time had come for them both.

He wrapped his hands around her waist and moved with her now, a synchronized pulse, as their bodies and hearts became one. Sarah called out his name, time and again, the constant assurance stroked his mind and he, too, called for her, the woman he had waited so long for. "Sarah."

They fell away and apart, shattered by the impact. But soon Sarah found her way back to him, and he did her. He held her tight in the crook of his arm, unmindful of his injuries, of the press of her head against his bruised chest. He wanted her there. He'd never let her go.

"You okay, sweetheart?" he asked, wondering if he'd lost too much control. Sarah was a new mother and he'd pressed himself to be patient and gentle with her.

She chuckled, a soft tiny sound that rumbled in her chest. "I was going to ask you the same question."

He smiled, kissing her forehead. "You can bruise me anytime, Sarah."

She shot her head up. "Did I—"

"No, you didn't. I was just stating a fact. Anytime you want to, feel free. I sure liked the way you kept me awake."

She laid her head back on his chest and relaxed, her soft hair tickling his chin. "Oh, Case. What now?"

"Now?" he repeated. He knew he wanted a life with Sarah. He knew he needed for her and the baby to be his family, in the true sense, but he feared Sarah might not be ready for that. He'd spent all this time, going slow, waiting for her. He couldn't rush her now. He couldn't tell what was in his heart. He couldn't chance her running again. "Now, you roll over so we both can get some sleep."

"But your head, Case. What about your concussion?"

"I'll be fine, darlin', but I'm completely beat. We both need to rest."

"Would you rest better in your own room?"

"Not a chance." Case wasn't ready to give up this time with Sarah. He wanted to hold her through the night, to wake up next to her in the morning and maybe make love again. But it had been a long night, and he was dog-tired. "Do you want me to go?"

Sarah gazed at him with warmth and shook her head. "No. I want you right here."

Relief registered and Case smiled. "Okay, then roll over lady or neither of us is going to get much sleep tonight. And that's a promise."

He noted a flash of her smile when she rolled over. Case sidled up next to her, threw his arm around her waist, and kissed her cheek. "Good night, sweet Sarah."

He knew he'd have good dreams tonight.

# Twelve

**M**orning sunshine brought forth recriminations. In the light of day, all that had transpired during the night plagued Sarah's thoughts. When she'd seen Case last night, standing in her doorway so badly beaten, a jolt of awareness shot through her at how very much she cared for him. He'd become an important part of her life even though she'd fought hard against it, but she knew now that he had the power to destroy her. Images of the old Case, teasing her, playing pranks on her, warred with the man she'd made love with last night.

For more than twenty years, she'd held no faith in Case Jarrett and all during that time, he'd done nothing to gain her trust. But since he'd come back to the ranch, things had somehow been different. Or was she just trying to rationalize now, since she'd made love with him? How could she be sure which man he really was?

Sarah eased herself out of bed, making sure not to

disturb Case. He looked vulnerable lying there, his dark hair falling onto his forehead, with scrapes on his face and battle marks on his body. She'd let him rest.

Sarah showered and dressed quietly then checked on Christiana. The baby cooed when she noticed her. "Hello, sweet baby. Mama's here."

Sarah nursed her, gave her a quick bath, then lifted her up and headed downstairs to the kitchen. The phone rang and Sarah picked it up before the second ring, so that the noise wouldn't disturb Case. "Hello."

"Hello, Mrs. Jarrett. This is Sheriff Pickley. I have good news for you. Thanks to Mr. Jarrett's description last night, we've apprehended a suspect. We found a man, who'd obviously been bloodied in a fight driving like a maniac on the Interstate. One of my deputies picked him up and the man made a full confession to the crimes in the area. His name is Ralph Wooden. Do you know him?"

Sarah didn't know him personally, but she'd seen him in town on occasion. "Wooden, yes. I've heard of him. He owns a place just outside of Barrel Springs, right?"

"Yes, that's right. Apparently his place was last on the list of ranches Beckman Corporation needed for the development to pass. Wooden's in debt up to his eyeballs and needed that deal to go through."

"Are you saying that he's responsible for McPherson's barn fire, and all the other crimes?"

"Yes, he's confessed to it all. Beckman Corporation had nothing to do with it. Wooden was pretty desperate. He figured he'd use intimidation to get landowners to sell. As I said, the man's on the edge. But we've got him now. There shouldn't be any more disturbances."

"Thank you, Sheriff. I'll be sure to pass on the news."

Sarah hung up the phone and sat down, absorbing it

all, wondering how a man could get so desperate that he'd put his neighbors at such risk. It was certain now that Beckman Corporation would cut their losses and leave Barrel Springs. All the other neighbors had held firm. They wouldn't sell out. Those land agents had to see it was a lost cause. They could plan their pricey development somewhere else.

When the phone rang again, Sarah jumped up to catch it on the first ring. A woman with a sultry voice asked to speak with Case.

"I'm sorry. He's not available right now. May I take a message?"

"Yes, tell him this is Julia and that I have to cancel tonight. But I do have something better planned. I'll call him back later with the details."

Sarah's mouth gaped open. Stunned into silence, she nodded into the phone then caught herself just in time. "All right, I'll tell him." With a shaky hand, Sarah hung up the phone. Suspicions of the worst kind crept in. She realized that today was Tuesday. The woman named Julia was canceling their Tuesday night. Sarah sat down before she fell down, her legs as wobbly as her mind at the moment.

Sarah tried a rational explanation. She tried to find a reason why Case left every Tuesday night without sharing where he was going. She tried to give Case the benefit of the doubt.

But Sarah couldn't do it. He hadn't earned that right.

Sarah hated what she was feeling, the mistrust, misgivings and suspicions. Unwelcome thoughts of past years came barreling forth of the Case Jarrett Sarah had known so well. Forgetting about all the other mean-spirited pranks he'd played, Case had done one unforgivable thing in Sarah's mind. He'd abandoned his brother when times were tough and if he hadn't, just maybe, Reid would still be alive today.

Images of last night flashed in her head. Sarah had made love to him, giving herself freely, openly, granting him her trust. She'd trusted him with her heart, a fragile heart that had been torn apart lately. Was Case that ruthless, that uncaring, to take from her the one thing that she'd protected with diligence and shatter it so cruelly?

Had Sarah just been an easy convenience to Case? He was living here with her so why not make love to the lonely widow? She was handy to have around when the mood struck. Case had made no claims of love or commitment to her. He hadn't said anything that even came close. Sarah bit back tears of frustration. Had she been a fool once again when it came to Case Jarrett?

Sarah knew she couldn't sort out any of this here, on the ranch. She couldn't look Case in the eye just now. She needed time and space away from him. Perhaps then, she could see more clearly and look deep into her heart for the answers.

Once decided what she would do, Sarah made short work of gathering up a few clothes and putting some things together for Christiana. She prayed Case would sleep most of the morning and this time her prayers had been answered. She managed to get out of the room and off the ranch in quick time.

The note she left for Case should explain everything.

Not twenty minutes later, Sarah knocked on Bobbi Sue's front door. Relief registered quickly when Bobbi Sue opened her door with a welcome smile. Teary-eyed, Sarah explained, "I need a friend right now and a place to stay."

The house seemed eerily quiet. Case rose just before noon, amazed that he'd slept so late. He moved with caution about the room as he dressed, and was instantly reminded of sore muscles, stiff joints and aches over half of his body.

The scent of Sarah's flowery perfume permeating her bedroom reminded him of their encounter last night, one that he'd never forget and one that made him happier than anything he could recall since the birth of little Christiana. Sarah had come to him last night out of desire, not need this time, and they'd made incredible love. Sarah was so much a part of him now that he couldn't imagine a life without her. Case smiled, thinking back on their tumultuous history. Who would have thought that after all they shared, all the heartache and losses that they would find their way to each other, on the ranch where he'd first laid eyes on her when she was just a child, some twenty years ago?

"Sarah," Case called out, but not too loudly to wake up Christie if she were still asleep. When he got no answer, he went searching to find neither Sarah nor the baby anywhere upstairs.

What he did find downstairs on the kitchen table was a note. His gut clenched, a sense of alarm bordering on anger, swept through him when he lifted the paper and read the words.

"Damn it, Sarah!" He crumpled the note in his fist and tossed it aside. "No way. I'm not letting you go. No way, lady."

It didn't matter to Case that Sarah said she needed time and space away from him. It didn't matter that Sarah was confused, that last night might have been a mistake. It didn't matter that Sarah had decided to leave the ranch for a while.

No. What mattered was the truth. And it was about

time that Sarah heard it all. Hell, he knew she didn't trust him. He knew she would be wary of his intentions, but he'd hoped to work through that, with her here, on the ranch as they went about their daily lives. Now, Case realized he had no choice, no other option but to confront her and confess everything.

Case grabbed his hat and truck keys and barreled out of the house. He knew just what he was going to say to Sarah, he'd been rehearsing the lines for months now. But Sarah had a stubborn streak and she might not listen. She might not want to hear the truth.

A short time later, with hat in hand, Case knocked on Bobbi Sue's front door. She opened up several moments later with a crying Christiana in her arms. "Case?"

"I've got to see Sarah, Bobbi Sue."

Bobbi Sue shook her head. "I'm sorry, Case. She's asked not to see you."

Little Christie's cries overshadowed their conversation and Bobbi Sue focused on the unhappy baby. "Oh, what's the matter, little one? Are you tired?"

Christie continued to cry. Case stepped inside the doorway. "Here, give her to me."

Bobbi Sue hesitated a moment and Case huffed out a sigh. "I know what to do."

Bobbi Sue relented, handing the baby over. Case cradled her head in his hand and held her along his arm so they could make eye contact. He spoke to her softly, calmly. "What's the matter, little beauty? Do you miss your uncle Case?" He rocked her in his arms. "Time to nap, I think." He continued rocking her until her eyes fought a losing battle and finally she closed them. Case rocked her a little longer until he was certain she was out then asked, "Where do you want to lay her down?"

Bobbi Sue ushered him inside and gestured to a small

quilt on her parlor floor. He set her down and kissed the top of Christie's head before lifting up to meet Bobbi Sue's gaze. "She should sleep awhile."

Bobbi Sue grinned. "Case, you're a natural with her. I'm impressed."

"Christie knows I love her, Bobbi Sue. She knows she can trust me. Now, I've just got to convince Sarah of that. Will you tell me where she is?"

Bobbi Sue glanced at Christie's sleeping form. "Look, I'm trying to be a good friend, but…well, I can see that maybe you should speak to Sarah. The three of you deserve a chance. But Case, you go easy on her, you got that?"

"I promise. The last thing I want is to hurt Sarah."

Bobbi Sue took in a deep breath and paused, running a hand down her face. For a moment Case worried that she'd changed her mind. "She's taking a walk down by the creek. She headed down the south path behind the house."

Case thanked Bobbi Sue, kissed her cheek and strode out the back door. In a few minutes, every truth Case had held deep inside since the night of Sarah's prom would be revealed.

Sarah leaned heavily against a cottonwood tree, gazing out onto the slow-moving creek, watching a shallow current of water make its way over rocks and fallen branches. The tree provided shady protection against the bright Arizona sunlight casting the gliding stream with a shiny glow that was almost too brilliant for the eyes. But even the beautiful surroundings didn't calm Sarah. So many thoughts crowded her mind, but the most important realization struck her hard, like a slap to her face. She'd realized it just now, as she blinked back the brightness of the day, and allowed her feelings to surface honestly, without qualm or interference from her brain.

She'd fallen in love with Case Jarrett.

And that could very well be her downfall.

"Sarah?"

She blinked, but didn't answer. She couldn't. Case stood close, just a few feet away. She heard the rustling of leaves as he'd come forward, but she didn't turn around.

"Sarah, we have to talk."

"I guess my wishes weren't important to you."

"I got your note."

"But you decided to do what you wanted anyway, regardless of my feelings."

"Hell, that's all I do care about, is your feelings. Don't condemn me for coming here. I had to. I'm crazy in love with you, Sarah. I couldn't stay away."

Sarah squeezed her eyes shut. His pronouncement surprised her. He claimed he loved her, but how could she believe him? There was so much mistrust between them. Just this morning, she'd had another jolt hearing that woman's voice asking for Case, breaking their date, but promising something better to come. Pride wouldn't allow Sarah to ask about her. If Case really loved her, he'd admit that he'd been involved with another woman. But no admissions came forth.

"I don't know what to say," Sarah admitted.

"Don't say anything, darlin', just listen. It's time you knew the truth. It's time I told you." Sarah heard Case take a deep breath, then let out a long sigh. "I've been in love with you for years, ever since the night of your senior prom."

Stunned, Sarah turned around sharply to face him. "What?"

She met his gaze and saw the truth in the dark depths of his eyes, the slow nod of his head. The truth not only astonished her but also frightened and confused her as well. "I fell head-over-heels, Sarah. When we kissed. You remember what it was like between us. God, I'd never felt anything like it in my life. It knocked me out completely and I realized that I was crazy about you. It was a hard road for me after that, realizing you'd thought I'd played a trick on you. I couldn't tell you the truth— that I hadn't been *playing* at anything. That what I felt was real and I'd fallen in love with you that night. Believe me, I didn't want to love you. You were Reid's girl and I did my best to hide my feelings, letting you think the worst of me. I knew you two would end up married. And when you did marry my brother, I faced a real tough decision. I could stay at the ranch and let it tear me up inside watching you two together, or I could leave."

Sarah's heart ached painfully. If she could believe Case then it explained so many things. "So you left."

"It was the only way for me, Sarah. I couldn't abide wanting my brother's wife. I left you two to your life. I managed, but I hated leaving Reid when he needed me. That part was the hardest. The guilt ate at me."

"He understood, Case. He never blamed you for that."

"I know. He told me when he was in the hospital. Sarah, there's something else you have to know. When I saw him, right before he died, he asked me to come home and watch out for you and the baby. I promised him I would."

Sarah's mind went numb learning that Reid had tried to provide for her and Christie even from his deathbed. She'd known he'd loved her very much, and this went a long way in proving it. Tears rained down her face. "He was such a good man."

Case agreed. "The best, Sarah. But you have to know I would have come back to the ranch even if he didn't ask me. I would have come back for you and the baby. I've loved you for a long time, Sarah. And I think you love me, too."

Overwhelmed by emotion, Sarah had trouble sorting through everything Case had said. She had trouble separating her love for Reid, and all they'd meant to each other, especially now, upon learning how much he'd worried about her, and her feelings for Case. It was all too fresh, too new. She needed time to let it all sink in.

"Sarah," Case pushed on, "there was always something between us."

"No, that's not true."

"Isn't it? What about the night of the prom? Hell, Sarah, if you recall, it went way beyond kissing that night. You called my name and that shocked me because of what we'd almost done. When we kissed, when did you know it was *me* and not Reid? It's a question I've asked myself a hundred times. But only you know the truth. I think you owe us, you, me and Christie the answer to that question."

Sarah wiped her tearstained face, anger boiling up. Case had no right asking that of her, making her recall that awful night. He had no right making her doubt her love for Reid. She'd loved Reid with all of her heart. She wouldn't allow Case to make her remember the emotions of a seventeen-year-old girl. She'd felt tremendous guilt that night, and for a long time afterward. Reid deserved more than that from her. And Sarah had a few questions of her own for Case. He was the one who couldn't be trusted, not her.

She raised her chin and met his gaze point blank. "I've got a question for you, Case. Why do you leave the ranch every Tuesday night? You never tell me where you're going or why? But there's a woman with a seductive voice who certainly knows.''

Case stepped back as though he'd been struck. His expression grim, he searched her eyes. They stared at each other a long time, neither one speaking, each seeming to weigh heavily the decisions to be made. It was clear to Sarah that he wouldn't grant her an answer to that question.

Finally Case pursed his lips and spoke with quiet determination. ''I think we both want the same thing, but until you're willing to see the truth, that's not going to happen. You can find me at the ranch, when you make your decision.''

Sarah watched as he turned and strode away. He didn't stop, or pause or turn around. Sarah stood, motionless, watching him walk away and realizing that she had her own demons to face. Case wanted her trust, her faith as well as her love. She had to look into her heart and come up with the truth Case had spoken about so vehemently.

The decision wouldn't come easy.

The next day, Sarah stood just inside the barn at the Triple R, facing facts and the man she'd fallen in love with. She'd searched her heart through the night countless times and each time, she had come away with only one answer. She had to tell Case the truth.

Dark eyes penetrated hers, his frame solid and stable as he stood by his workbench, watching her, patiently waiting.

*Don't be a coward, Sarah. Tell him.*

''The minute our lips met, I knew,'' Sarah admitted, finally. ''I knew it was you the night of the prom, Case.''

Sarah had fought off her own demons last night. She

knew Case deserved the truth. He deserved so much more than that. Since coming back to the Triple R, he'd been there for her at every turn, helping put the ranch back together financially, delivering her beloved child, risking his life to protect her, time and again. Her grandmother's ring, so precious to Sarah, sat in a blue velvet ring box on her dresser, because of Case and the sacrifices he'd been willing to make.

Sarah had uncovered the truth about Case Jarrett. She'd discovered who he really was and found him to be a man worthy of her love. She'd been hard on him, recalling past hurts rather than regarding his unselfish deeds of late with any credence or gratitude. Sarah hadn't been fair to him and she wondered if he'd even want her anymore.

He studied her a moment, setting aside his tools at the workbench. Heart pounding, Sarah approached Case slowly. "I knew, Case. And it scared me. I put all the blame on you that night. Unfairly. But what I felt that night had been so intense," she stated, releasing the guilt and pain she'd harbored, "that I couldn't face the truth. I *loved* Reid."

Hard eyes, softened on her as he came closer. "I know you did."

"And what happened that night made me doubt myself and everything I'd always believed. I couldn't doubt my love for Reid, ever, so I blamed it all on you."

"And now?" Case's entire expression changed, alighting his face with hope, giving Sarah the courage to confess all. She stood boot to boot with him, gazing up into his wonderfully dark eyes, seeing perhaps, a second chance for them both and a new future.

"And now?" Sarah repeated on a soft whisper, "I

realize that I was wrong about you and...and I'm pretty much head-over-heels in love with you, too.''

Case's grin splintered his beautiful face and widened bruises that were still healing. "Sarah," he said swooping her into his arms and crushing her with a soul-searing kiss. He held her tight, squeezing with gentleness, making her feel cherished, treasured, fully and completely loved. Sarah surrendered to him granting him her trust, giving him her heart, no longer afraid to place her faith in him.

When they broke apart, Case was smiling, joy washing over his face. Sarah, too, couldn't help her silly grin. She peered over his shoulder to his workbench and something caught her eye.

Taking his hand, she walked over to the work area and lifted up a newly framed certificate. "What's this?"

"I was going to surprise you with it, darlin'," Case confessed, standing behind her and brushing a soft kiss along her throat. Sarah fought the urge to turn in his arms and kiss him again. Her curiosity had gotten the best of her.

Instead Sarah read the words imprinted on the certificate. "It says Boot Camp. You went to Boot Camp, Case?"

A crooked knowing smile curled his lips up. "Uh-huh. Tuesday nights. Boot Camp for New Daddies. And I passed with flying colors."

*Boot Camp for New Daddies?*

Awed by his admission and new dawning knowledge, everything suddenly became perfectly clear. Case had been going to classes on Tuesday nights, for her, for the baby. He hadn't been involved in anything illicit. No, the hot steamy dates she'd imagined hadn't been that at all. Heavens, the man had been learning how to burp and diaper the baby. The backs of Sarah's eyes burned with fresh tears. "You did that…for us?"

On a deep breath, Case nodded. "I didn't know a darn thing about babies and I wanted to be a good father for little Christie."

"Oh, Case." Sarah's heart stirred and she realized she'd been right in placing her faith in him. "You're a wonderful father, already."

Case took her into his arms once again, lowering them down onto an untied bale of hay. "I am?"

Sarah lay beside him, embraced by his protective arms. "Uh-huh," she breathed out, fingering the scar on his face, a symbol reflecting the differences in the two men she'd loved, each one being good, solid and sure, but so very different. Sarah said a prayer of thanks for the gift of a second chance, for a man she would love forever. "Yes, you're pretty wonderful."

He kissed her lips gently. "How'd you think I'd be in the husband department?"

"Husband?" Hope surged through her body, filling her with immense joy.

"I need you for my wife, Sarah. Marry me. Be my family."

Sarah wanted nothing more. A sense of peace settled around her and she knew without a doubt that this was the right decision. She needed Case in her life. She'd found the true heart of this cowboy and he was all she could ever ask for in a man. "Yes. I'll marry you. We'll be your family, Case."

"I love you, Sarah Jarrett."

"And I love you, Case Jarrett."

Case drew from her lips, kissing her until she thought she'd die from want. His fingers worked the tiny pearl buttons on her flowery dress. "One important thing I've learned at Camp. Take advantage of baby's sleep time. What's our little girl doing?''

''Sleeping at Bobbi Sue's,'' Sarah responded with eager anticipation.

A sexy smile lifted the corners of Case's very kissable mouth. He covered her body with his, ready to make love to her, ready to claim her as his, ready to sear their hearts as one. ''I was hoping you'd say that, sweetheart.''

# Epilogue

Sarah bent to lay flowers on Reid's grave. The bunched wildflowers rested on the headstone without disturbance. Not a flutter or sound disrupted the quiet solitude of the hillside. Case stood at a distance dressed in his dark suit and black string tie, looking every bit the new groom, holding a wiggling Christiana in his strong arms. And Sarah knew the exact moment her husband came up to stand beside her. She sensed his presence, the power and strength in him before his hand came to caress her shoulder.

"You know, I think Reid is okay with this," he said softly.

Sarah drew in a breath slowly, nodding, certain Case was right in his thinking. With head bent and voice somber, Case spoke quietly toward the grave, "Nobody will love them more. I'll take care of them until I draw my last breath."

Tears stung Sarah's eyes and she folded herself into her husband's embrace. Out of the quiet, cottonwood leaves rustled, glinting in the sunlight, without benefit of a breeze.

Sarah peered up at the solid ancient tree and smiled. "Yes, I think Reid is really okay with this."

\*  \*  \*  \*  \*

*If you enjoyed*
THE HEART OF A COWBOY,
*you will love Charlene's next book, coming*
*next month from Harlequin Historicals:*
THE LAW AND KATE MALONE
*by Charlene Sands*

*Available February 2003*

*Don't miss it!*

If you enjoyed what you just read,
then we've got an offer you can't resist!

# Take 2 bestselling love stories FREE!

# Plus get a FREE surprise gift!

# COMING NEXT MONTH

**#1489 SLEEPING BEAUTY'S BILLIONAIRE—Caroline Cross**
*Dynasties: The Barones*
Years ago, Colleen Barone's mother had pressured her into breaking up with Gavin O'Sullivan. Then Colleen saw her gorgeous former flame at a wedding, and realized the old chemistry was still there. But the world-famous hotel magnate seemed to think she only wanted him now that he was rich. Somehow, Colleen had to convince Gavin she truly loved him—mind, body and soul!

**#1490 KISS ME, COWBOY!—Maureen Child**
After a bitter divorce, the last thing sexy single dad Mike Fallon wanted was to get romantically involved again. But when feisty Nora Bailey seemed determined to lose her virginity—with the town Casanova, no less—Mike rushed to her rescue. He soon found himself drowning in Nora's baby blues, but she wanted a husband. And he wasn't husband material…or was he?

**#1491 THAT BLACKHAWK BRIDE—Barbara McCauley**
*Secrets!*
Three days before her wedding, debutante Clair Beauchamp learned from handsome investigator Jacob Carver that she was really a Blackhawk from Texas. Realizing her whole life, including her almost-marriage, was a lie, Clair asked Jacob to reunite her with her family. But the impromptu road trip led to the consummation of their passionate attraction, and soon Clair yearned to make their partnership permanent.

**#1492 CHARMING THE PRINCE—Laura Wright**
Time was running out; if Prince Maxim Thorne didn't find a bride, his father would find one for him. So Max set out to seduce the lovely Francesca Charming, certain his father would never agree to his marrying a commoner and would thus drop his marriage demand. But what started out as make-believe turned into undeniable passion…. Might marrying Francesca give Max the fairy-tale ending he hadn't known he wanted?

**#1493 PLAIN JANE & THE HOTSHOT—Megan McKinney**
*Matched in Montana*
Shy Joanna Lofton met charismatic smoke-jumping firefighter Nick Kramer while on a mountain retreat. Joanna worried she wasn't exciting enough for a man like Nick, but her fears proved unfounded, for the fires raging around them couldn't compare to the flame of attraction burning between them.

**#1494 AT THE TYCOON'S COMMAND—Shawna Delacorte**
When Kim Donaldson inherited a debt to Jared Stevens's family, she agreed to work as Jared's assistant for the summer. Despite a generations-old family feud, as Kim and Jared worked together, their relationship took a decidedly romantic turn. But could they put the past behind them before it tore them apart?

SDCNM0103